The Bucktails' Shenandoah March

William P. Robertson (signature)

by
William P. Robertson
and
David Rimer

W M KIDS 12

WHITE MANE KIDS
SHIPPENSBURG, PENNSYLVANIA

This White Mane Books publication
was printed by
Beidel Printing House, Inc.
63 West Burd Street
Shippensburg, PA 17257-0708 USA

The acid-free paper used in this book meets the guidelines for permanence and durability of the Committee on Production Guidelines for Book Longevity of the Council on Library Resources.

For a complete list of available publications
please write
White Mane Books
Division of White Mane Publishing Company, Inc.
P.O. Box 708
Shippensburg, PA 17257-0708 USA

Library of Congress Cataloging-in-Publication Data

Robertson, William P.
    The Bucktails' Shenandoah march / by William P. Robertson and David Rimer.
        p. cm. -- (White mane kids)
    Includes bibliographical references (p.).
    Summary: Under Kane's able leadership, the tenacious Bucktails once again face the Rebs as they fight their way from their winter camp, through the Shenandoah Valley, and on toward Alexandria, Virginia.
    ISBN 1-57249-293-7 (alk. paper)
        1. Kane, Thomas Leiper, 1822-1883--Juvenile fiction. [1. Kane, Thomas Leiper, 1822-1883--Fiction. 2. United States. Army. Pennsylvania Infantry Regiment, 42nd (1861-1864)--Fiction. 3. United States--History--Civil War, 1861-1865--Fiction. 4. War--Fiction.] I. Rimer, David. II. Title. III. WM kids.

PZ7.R54913 Bu 2002
[Fic]--dc21

                                                                    2002016867

PRINTED IN THE UNITED STATES OF AMERICA

Contents

***
iii

Authors' Note

The Bucktails' Shenandoah March was written with a conscious effort to accurately portray historical events in the chronology of their happening. Further, the authors have used portions of dialogue attributed to the real-life officers who participated in the events related in the book. Although many of the characters and their actions are fictitious, the story is told with an eye to the illustrious history of the Pennsylvania Bucktails.

Tom Aaron of Company K, 1st Pennsylvania Rifles, displays his skirmishing skills during the 2001 Armed Forces Day activities at Driftwood, Pennsylvania.

Acknowledgments

The authors would like to thank MARCIA RIMER, STEPHANIE RIMER, and SUE CARLETTA for their technical help in producing this novel. Thanks also go out to local historians PAUL ROBERTSON and RICHARD ROBERTSON for assisting with the research. RICH ADAMS, commander of the Bucktail reenactment regiment, also deserves applause for his helpfulness. Visit Rich's Web site at http://www.pabucktail.com for a list of the regiment's activities and for historical information about the famous Civil War sharpshooters. All photographs were taken by WILLIAM P. ROBERTSON unless otherwise noted. Many thanks to CAPTAIN CHUCK COPELLO and the members of Company K for participating in the photo shoot. Finally, HAROLD COLLIER, ALEXIS HANDERAHAN, NICOLE RILEY, MARIANNE ZINN, VICKI STOUFFER, DENISE LOGAN, and all the other nice folks at White Mane Publishing merit a tip of the hat.

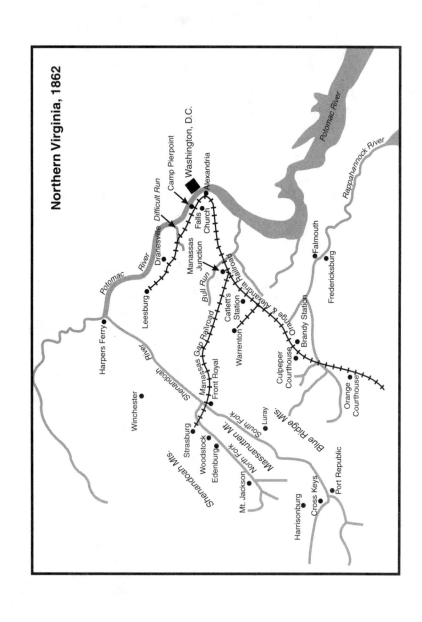

Northern Virginia, 1862

Potomac River

Rappahannock River

Camp Pierpoint
Washington, D.C.
Alexandria

Difficult Run
Dranesville
Falls Church

Potomac River

Manassas Junction

Bull Run

Leesburg

Orange & Alexandria Railroad

Catlett's Station

Warrenton

Falmouth

Fredericksburg

Harpers Ferry

Shenandoah River

Manassas Gap Railroad

Front Royal

Brandy Station

Culpeper Courthouse

Orange Courthouse

Winchester

South Fork
Luray

Blue Ridge Mts.

Strasburg
Woodstock
Edenburg
Mt. Jackson

North Fork

Massanutten Mt.

Shenandoah Mts.

Harrisonburg
Cross Keys
Port Republic

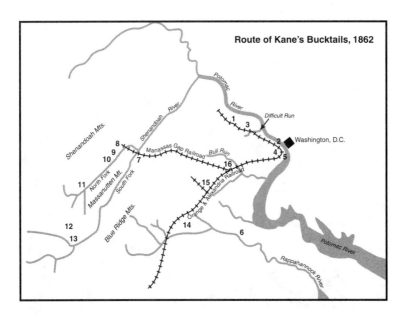

Route of Kane's Bucktails, 1862

1. Dec. 20, 1861—Bucktails defeat Rebels at Battle of Dranesville.
2. Dec. 1861–Mar. 1862—Bucktails winter at Camp Pierpont, Langley, Va.
3. Mar. 10—Bucktails camp at Hunter's Mills after leaving Camp Pierpont.
4. Mar. 15—Bucktails camp at Falls Church.
5. Mar. 16–Apr. 9—Bucktails in Alexandria expecting to be shipped to the Peninsula; regiment reunited here in Sept. and Kane promoted to general.
6. Apr. 28–May 23—Bucktails camp at Falmouth where reviewed by President Lincoln; regiment split, with four companies following Kane to the Shenandoah and six companies following Major Stone to the Peninsula.
7. May 31—Bucktails arrive at Front Royal as part of Bayard's Flying Brigade.
8. June 1—Kane's Bucktails fail to capture Jackson's wagon train at Strasburg.
9. June 2—Kane's Bucktails camp at Woodstock after 18 miles of skirmish duty.
10. June 3—Rebels burn Stony Creek bridge at Edenburg.
11. June 3—Rebels burn bridge over North Fork of the Shenandoah River.
12. June 6—Bucktails lose to the Rebels at Harrisonburg; Kane wounded/captured.
13. June 8—Bucktails rescue Union battery at Cross Keys.
14. Aug. 19—Kane rejoins Bucktails at Brandy Station.
15. Aug. 22—Kane's Bucktails drive off J.E.B. Stuart's cavalry at Catlett's Station.
16. Aug. 30—Kane's Bucktails aid Union retreat at Second Battle of Bull Run.

Meet the Company K Bucktail Reenactors who posed for photos in this book. The original Company K members were from Clearfield County and fought under Major Roy Stone in the Peninsula campaign.

Standing, *left to right*: Captain Chuck Copello, Jim Drexler, Brian Ickes, Tom Aaron, Jessie Moyer, Ron Armstrong, and Clarence Walker. Sitting, *left to right*: Brent Armstrong and Matt Baldwin.

Chapter One

BUCKTAIL CITY

A jockey-sized Union officer and his two aides rode at a deliberate pace along a rutted road in the Virginia countryside. Winter's snow had mixed with the rich soil to create a thick, red mud that muffled the usual clop of the horses' hooves. Along either side of the road, the terrain showed well-tended farms with wood fences, substantial barns, and fallow fields.

If it wasn't for this stinking mud, thought the officer, this scene would make a beautiful woodcut to display over my home hearth. How it contrasts with the hell of this war.

The officer's face was gaunt beneath a black beard that was combed to conceal the red line of a fresh battle scar. He was still not completely healed from his wound, and the jarring of his horse's trot caused him to grit his teeth in pain.

"Sir, perhaps a brief rest would be in order," suggested one of the aides, noting his commander's grimace. "We've ridden for quite a spell."

"Not yet," replied the officer. "Camp Pierpont can't be too far now. I'd like to arrive before nightfall and check on my men."

"But Lieutenant Colonel," cautioned the other aide, "wouldn't it be better if you rested at least—"

"That's enough, Sergeant. Let's ride."

1

The soldiers continued on in silence until a sentry stepped out from behind a tree and commanded harshly, "Riders, halt and identify yerselves."

"Open your eyes, soldier," grunted the officer testily. "Don't you recognize the man who led you into battle at Dranesville?"

"Why . . . Why, it is you. Sorry, Lieutenant Colonel. It's a mighty dark evenin' an'—"

"No need to apologize, son, for doing your duty. Even though the mud has ended troop movement until spring, it doesn't hurt to be cautious. You're doing a fine job here, Private. Now, could you direct me to headquarters?"

"My pleasure, sir," said the sentry with a smart salute. "Jess go straight down this here street. It's the big wall tent ta the left. Glad ta have ya back, Lieutenant Colonel, sir."

The lieutenant colonel returned the sentry's salute and rode off down the street followed by his aides. When they had reached headquarters and dismounted, the officer said, "That ride has made me stiffer than my month in bed at the hospital. I need to take a walk and stretch my legs. Tend to the horses, men, and tell the duty officer I've arrived. When I get back, we'll find some housing. First, I need to see if our regiment is comfortably situated."

After the aides had saluted and gone to check in with the duty officer, the lieutenant colonel sloshed along the muddy streets of Camp Pierpont, staring at the squares of tents occupied by the various regiments. The January night was chilly, and his lungs rebelled against the dampness.

The officer approached a sentry posted at the intersection of two streets, and the soldier snapped to attention and then stood shivering in the ankle-deep mud.

"Private, do you know where the Bucktail Regiment is bivouacked?" asked the officer, coughing into a gloved hand.

"Yes, sir, Lieutenant Colonel. Bucktail City is that little log village to the right. You can't miss it. Them riflemen worked like beavers when they arrived in camp an' built them barracks jess as quick as you please. The rest of us is stuck livin' in tents. But not them boys."

"Thank you, Private," replied the officer, fighting back a knowing smile.

Following the sentry's directions, the lieutenant colonel entered a complex of small huts that he studied with interest. The sides of these barracks were built of logs while the pointed roofs were constructed of canvas. Each hut had a stone fireplace in one corner with a chimney of sod built on top. Although most of the quarters were only four or five feet high, the officer could see that they provided excellent protection from the elements.

In the crowded center of Bucktail City, Sibley tents sprouted between the log barracks. These tents always reminded the lieutenant colonel of Indian wigwams, and he figured they were set up to accommodate the new recruits that had arrived while he was recovering. He was anxious to see what kind of men had been sent to replace the brave Bucktails killed or wounded at the battle of Dranesville.

Near these wigwams, the officer stopped to fight a wave of nausea that made the epaulets jerk on his shoulders. While he waited for the convulsions to pass, he was startled by a familiar voice that boomed from the tent to his left.

"What do ya mean ya ain't gonna vote fer Thomas Kane?" growled the soldier.

"Well, I jess think that Hugh McNeil would make a better colonel."

"Is that so?" scoffed another voice. "Don't ya know that Lieutenant Colonel Kane was the fella that organized this here regiment in the first place?"

"Yeah," added a third soldier, "without him we'da never come up with the Bucktail insignia neither."

"This e-lection wouldn't be needed if Colonel Biddle hadn't gone off an' become a congressman," grumbled the dissenter. "Why, Biddle knew all about whippin' troops inta shape. Kane always messed up drills that even the dumbest hayseed knew by heart. We'da never got trained proper with Kane in command."

"Now wait a gol-dang minute," bellowed the first soldier. "If Biddle was so good at trainin' fellas, what happened ta you?"

"An' where was the great Biddle when them Reb Minie balls was whizzin' an' snappin' 'round us at Dranesville?" asked still another Bucktail. "Lieutenant Colonel Kane wasn't paradin' 'round Washington. He was with us all along, fightin' like a wildcat. Kane acted like them bullets was harmless as blowflies when he led the charge that scattered them Rebs."

"Gettin' shot in the face the way he done only makes me think that Kane is more reckless than brave. An' don't ya remember last summer when he disobeyed Biddle an' took our scoutin' party way beyond the support of the regiment? You fellas are fools if ya elect Kane fer our colonel."

"An' you're a coward if ya don't. What'd ya expect ta do when you joined this here army? Drill in some camp behind the lines er find the Rebs an' fight 'em?"

A deep growl rumbled from inside the tent, followed by fists striking flesh. The ailing officer barely had time to step back before the tent flap sliced open and a burly sergeant came spilling out onto the street grappling with a wiry, little private. The antagonists were followed by ten rumpled-looking soldiers who formed a circle and cheered on the combatants like it was a schoolyard fight.

With the private punching for the big man's groin, the antagonists rolled over and over until they were both completely covered with mud. Finally, the bigger man used his knees to pin his squirming opponent to the ground. He raised a ham hand to smash the wiry soldier in the mouth when the newly arrived officer stepped forward and commanded, "That's enough, Sergeant Curtis. Let him up." Upon recognizing the sharp voice, a wave of disappointment swept over the sergeant's face, followed by a worried expression. Curtis stood up, yanked his antagonist to his feet, and turned to give a crude salute. "Lieutenant Colonel Kane, sir," he exclaimed. "Good ta have ya back, sir."

At the mention of the officer's name and rank, the rumpled-looking soldiers jostled into a ragged line in front of their tent. Beside Curtis and the muddy private stood a bespectacled, young man with broad Scandinavian features. Next was a sinewy Indian lad and two lanky woodsmen, who grinned good-naturedly. These soldiers were flanked by a slack-jawed private; a short, sullen man in his thirties; and an overweight, ruddy-faced corporal. An awed drummer boy and two owl-eyed recruits formed up at the end of the line. Like the rest of the unit, these new men wore dark blue tunics and kepi caps decorated with deer hide.

Lieutenant Colonel Kane surveyed the troops gravely but then said with a wry grin, "Well, at least I see that the battle at Dranesville didn't take the fight out of you, Sergeant Curtis."

"Sorry, sir. But I was only campaignin' fer—"

"I heard, Sergeant. Still I can't allow brawling among my troops. And I also can't allow you to beat up someone because his opinion differs from yours. Captain McNeil is a fine officer and gentleman. Although I appreciate your support, Hosea Curtis, each man must be free to vote the way he chooses. Understood?"

"Yes, sir. But Starr—"

"Good," Kane admonished. "You also have to understand that every leader has his strengths and weaknesses. Colonel

Biddle is a veteran of the Mexican War and a professional soldier. That's why I gave up the colonelcy to him when we organized this regiment."

"Yeah, but you got more starch than him," interrupted one of the lanky woodsmen with a gap-toothed grin. "We'd follow ya ta hell an' back, sir."

"Thank you. Private Crossmire, isn't it?"

"You can call me Boone, sir," volunteered Crossmire. "Everybody else does."

"Thank you, Boone. But as I was saying, every Bucktail must decide for himself who'd be best suited to lead this regiment. McNeil proved his mettle, too, when we crossed into Virginia and engaged the Confederates. At Dranesville he even commanded you boys for a short time while I had charge of the brigade."

"Beg your pardon, sir," interrupted the bespectacled private. "I just want to say that you have the support of Company I. We've been with you since you signed us up in Smethport, and we're going to stick with you no matter what. We're your Bucktails, sir."

"Private Jewett . . . Private Culp," Kane said, recalling the faces of the young lads of the company. "I don't doubt your loyalty or your fighting spirit one bit after seeing how you handled yourselves in battle."

"Let's hear it for the colonel, men," shouted Sergeant Curtis. "Hip. Hip. Hurrah! Hip. Hip. Hurrah!"

When the cheers had died down, Kane, suppressing a smile, said, "Let's not get ahead of ourselves. I'm still your *lieutenant* colonel."

"Yeah, at least until the e-lection, day after tomorrow," shouted Frank Crandall. "We's all with ya, sir."

"That's all of us 'cept him," grunted Sergeant Curtis, pointing toward the muddy, little private, who had begun to edge toward the tent during the other men's celebration.

"By the way, Private," said Lieutenant Colonel Kane, fixing the man with his hawkish eyes. "I don't remember seeing you at Dranesville. And I don't remember dismissing you, either. What is your name?"

"Jeb Starr, sir," replied the soldier, squirming uneasily. "I got separated from the unit before the charge. I used to be a cobbler up Littleton way an' ain't been out in the woods much."

"Fer a cobbler, he sure don't take much care o' his boots," Boone observed, pointing at Starr's split brogans. "Think he'd at least stitch 'em up as wet as it's been."

"Well, Starr," said Kane with a withering glare, "I hope for your sake that you watch your step better in the future. And take care of those boots like Boone advised. *Now* you're dismissed."

Starr, followed by the slack-jawed private, ducked into the tent before anyone else could insult him. The rest of the soldiers swarmed around Kane to wish him luck and further assure him of their support.

When Curtis' squad returned to their bedrolls, the object of their scorn appeared to be asleep next to his friend. Although the sergeant had to stoop to circle the cramped quarters, he still managed to give Starr a boot in the ribs while going back to his blanket. The private grunted softly but showed no further sign of consciousness.

"Gol-dang it," howled Curtis. "Why didn't they make these here Sibley tents big enough ta move around proper? They ain't nothin' but glorified teepees fit fer savages."

"Hey, not everybody has trouble gettin' 'round in here," winked Boone. "Starr an' Miles do jess fine. 'Course, they's both scrawny runts."

"Fun-ny," replied Curtis. "I jess wish we hadn't a-rrived here at Camp Pierpont a week late on account of that scoutin' duty Captain Blanchard give us. Then we'd be sleepin' nice an' cozy in our own log hut instead o' sharin' a tent with weasels an' stinkin' recruits. It still burns my bacon that there ain't enough room left in Bucktail City fer us ta build our own barracks. Why, we's jess as good as the other veterans of our regiment, but they ain't stuck in no tents."

"Ah, Hosea, it ain't that bad," said Frank.

"An' look at that gol-dang stove," ranted the sergeant. "Bein' cone shaped, it takes up half the standin' room we got. If we hadn't built a stone oven, it'd be useless fer cookin', too."

"At least it throws off some heat," said the bespectacled private, Jimmy Jewett. "We'd have been awful cold this winter without it."

"Ah, go suck an egg. An' while you're at it, throw in a couple more logs, an' get yerself ta sleep. Mornin' comes mighty early 'round here."

"An' you kin bet with Kane back, we'll be the ones wakin' the roosters," chuckled Boone.

The Sibley tent was twelve feet high in the center and eighteen feet in diameter. The stove was in the middle of the floor, which forced the men to sleep with their boots toward it. Bucky, the Indian lad, watched the sparks kick up inside the firebox when Jimmy opened the stove door and shoved some green logs inside. After Bucky traced the course of the stovepipe up through the opening in the sooty canvas ceiling, he warily moved his bedroll to his usual spot in front of the tent entrance.

"What's wrong, Bucky?" asked Boone Crossmire, lying down beside him. "Does the heatin' o' this here fine canvas hotel make ya nervous? I bet General McDowell hisself don't have finer accom-modations."

"I don't like bein' crowded in here with so many other soldiers," confessed the Indian boy. "An' that stove scares me. I guess I'm jess used ta sleepin' in a log cabin with a proper-built fireplace er in the wide-open spaces o' the woods. If that canvas ever does ketch fire, I'll be outside so fast—"

"Yeah, but I'll be the first one out the flap," assured Boone. "I kin move mighty quick with my be-hind blazin'."

"Will you pipe down?" growled Curtis from across the tent. He was having a tough time wrapping his six-foot, five-inch frame in a wool blanket and getting comfortable on the damp ground. He kept inching closer to the stove until he finally settled into an uneasy slumber. He continued to shiver until his feet rested against the iron firebox. Before long, his boots started to smoke and his blanket to smolder. Then the smoldering wool burst into flames, and the sergeant was rolling to and fro over the soldiers on either side of him, spreading the fire to their blankets. The smoke and howling became terrific until Frank Crandall leaped forward to douse the blaze with a bucket of icy drinking water.

While Bucky and Boone scrambled out the tent flap gasping for air, Private Starr started awake, coughing violently. He peered through the smoke until he saw his soaked, singed sergeant hopping around the stove. Starr wheezed and choked back a laugh until the tears ran down his gaunt face.

"Gol-dang it, Starr. What's so hi-larious?" cursed Curtis, shaking off the water like a wet spaniel. "Look at my charred trousers. An' my blanket. Why, it's half gone."

"Mine, too," screeched one of the owl-eyed privates. "How could ya have set me on fire like that, Sergeant?"

"I didn't do it on purpose, you hayseed. I was jess rollin' ta put out my burnin' pant legs."

"Well, as I see it, there's only one solution to this here problem," shouted Boone through the tent flap. "Sergeant, you an' yer good friend Starr are gonna have ta share bedrolls."

Chapter Two

THE BLIZZARD

Bucky awoke well before dawn and listened to the wind howl through Camp Pierpont like a troop of phantom cavalry. The fire had burned down to coals, and he shivered in his blanket, afraid to open the stove hatch and throw in more wood. There was something about the glowing firebox that reminded Bucky of an Iroquois evil spirit that his pa always threatened to feed him to if he misbehaved. The spirit breathed flames, had an unquenchable appetite for human flesh, and was fed by a hundred hands. Nightmares of this monster had racked Bucky's sleep since he'd been confined to the Sibley tent of winter camp.

The Indian lad waited well past time for reveille, but no bugle blew. Finally, he loosened the tent flap and peered into the half-light. Outside a blizzard raged, and Bucky couldn't see the log barracks across the street for the wind-driven snow. Already drifts were almost even with the top of the tent opening. Bucky retied the flap, fighting back the fear of being snowbound that worried every man who had ever trapped and hunted for a living.

The cold draft that accompanied Bucky's curiosity caused a chain reaction of shivering and cursing among his tent mates. Finally, Sergeant Curtis, looking like a half-frozen corpse, sat up and muttered, "Gol-dang fire musta burned down ta nothin'. Starr, wasn't it yer turn ta keep it goin' last night?"

Jeb Starr was still sound asleep, and Curtis stood up and gave the private a kick to rouse him. After the sergeant repeated his question, Starr groaned softly before scrambling guiltily from his blanket. Still half asleep, he flung open the stove door and piled in so many logs that he extinguished the few remaining embers.

When the fire went out altogether, the sergeant bellowed, "You gotta be the biggest fool in Mr. Lincoln's army. I think ya done that on purpose, Starr, so I'd catch my death o' pneumonia. First, my gol-dang blanket burns up. Then, Crandall dang near drowns me. Now, ya go an' put out the fire!"

Red-faced, Starr yanked the logs out of the firebox, loaded it with pine twigs, and struck sparks from pieces of flint until the twigs smoldered and burst into flame. Afterward, he piled on some bigger twigs and some small kindling wood. When the tent was toasty again, Sergeant Curtis ordered Frank Crandall and Boone to prepare breakfast in the stone oven they had built below the stove.

While Frank and Boone set to work on their cooking chores, Curtis pulled on his coat, wormed through the tent flap, and waded through the snow to headquarters. The drifts were already up to his knees, and the sergeant cursed the blizzard under his breath as he battled his way through Bucktail City and across the buried parade ground.

At headquarters Captain Taylor of Company H, Captain McDonald of Company G, and several officers Curtis didn't recognize were singing a humorous ditty and laughing like snowbound lads celebrating a school closing. The officers were sipping brandy, and the sergeant licked his lips like a begging dog when he reported to his own Captain Blanchard for instructions. Knowing full well that enlisted men weren't permitted the indulgence of alcohol, he received his orders and returned to his men in an even fouler mood than before. He did manage, though, to get the accommodating Captain Taylor to scribble down the words to the lively song that amused the officers so much.

Sergeant Curtis entered with a blast of wind as the other soldiers crowded around the stove to eat. "Ain't no training again, boys," he grumbled. "Yesterday, they canceled drills because o' the mud. Now, because o' the blizzard. If this keeps up, we's gonna be too soft ta even fight among ourselves."

"Or too fat," chuckled Boone, nudging the pudgy corporal who stood next to him wolfing down a second baked potato.

"I ain't too fat ta whip yer scrawny be-hind," threatened Corporal Comfort.

"Hey, I was only funnin'. I jess hope ya don't get too porky ta hide behind a tree. That'd make ya an easy target fer them Rebs."

"This sure has been a crazy winter," said Frank. "I guess I jess can't get used ta havin' more rain than snow. Before today I can't remember one other time that the snow was over two inches deep."

"An' that always turned back inta mud as soon as the sun come out," complained the corporal.

"This Virginia is a mixed-up place alright," quipped Boone. "Why, the mud here is deeper than the snow in McKean County."

"I'm kinda glad we did get this here blizzard," sighed Frank. "I look out at it an' almost think I'm home where I belong."

"Speaking of home," said Jimmy, "I just got a letter yesterday from my mother. She said that all it's done in Smethport is snow. The drifts are so deep that people are having a hard time getting to church on Sunday. Attendance also has been down because of the war—"

"Hey, Jimmy," interrupted the drummer boy Sam Whalen. "A-A-Are you gonna write a letter to my ma like you p-p-promised? There'd be time now that we ain't d-d-drillin'."

"Sure, come over here and sit down on my bedroll."

"Hey, ya promised ta learn me some more readin', too," said Boone.

"Come on. School is in session," joked Jimmy.

Jimmy folded his blanket and spread it on the ground. He fished some paper, a bottle of ink, and a steel pen from his haversack and, flanked by Sam and Boone, sat down and placed the lid of a hardtack box on his knees. This served as his writing desk, and he held a piece of paper on it and wrote at the top "January, Camp Pierpont." Jimmy said and spelled each word while Boone dutifully repeated them at Jimmy's direction.

Sam was a wan boy of twelve. He had dark hair and the harried eyes of a trapped animal. He was so thin that most of the men called him Scarecrow. Even the smallest uniform hung on him like a horse blanket. His oversized cap slipped down over his ears, and he kept adjusting it the whole time he watched Jimmy.

"What do you want me to say to your mother, Sam?"

"I don't know, Jimmy. There ain't been much goin' on."

"How can you say that? In the past two days we've only had a fight, a fire, and a blizzard, not to mention the return of Lieutenant Colonel Kane. Any of that would make interesting news for your folks back home."

"An' don't fergit ta say what a fightin' wildcat she has fer a son," laughed Boone. "You could tell her that Sam captured Stonewall Jackson singlehanded an' pulled on Old Jack's beard 'til he yelled 'uncle' an' cried hisself ta sleep."

"D-D-Don't s-s-say that. T-T-That'd be a l-l-lie. You know I jess g-g-got here a coupla weeks ago with them other r-r-recruits. An' d-d-don't m-m-mention the f-f-fight or f-f-fire. That'd w-w-worry M-M-Ma to death. W-W-Why d-d-don't you tell her about this here camp. T-T-That'd be good. An' that I m-m-miss her."

"Okay, here it goes:

January
Camp Pierpont

Dear Mother,
    I arrived safe and sound at Camp Pierpont in Virginia. I can't believe I'm in another state. I'm with Company I of the Pennsylvania Bucktails. They've been in battle. They beat the Confederates at Dranesville, so I'm with veterans.
    The food is very good, and there's plenty of beef, bread, and bacon. We take turns cooking. Getting firewood is a problem, but we take turns at that, too.
    We have a big election coming up. We are to elect a new colonel. We want Lieutenant Colonel Kane to win because he cares for his men and started the regiment at Smethport, not so far from home.
    I'll tell you about the men in my outfit later. But for now I'd like to introduce Jimmy, who is writing this letter for me. He learned to write at the Smethport school, and he also loved studying about the Constitution. He hopes to be a lawyer some day.
    The weather here is a lot warmer than it is at home, and the whole camp is usually a big mud puddle. Other than the drifts caused by last night's blizzard, there has been very little snow.
    We drilled a lot before it got too muddy. I didn't mind, though, because my drum controls all the regiment's movements. I must be right or men could die.
    Right now my biggest battles are on the checkerboard. So far, I'm the company's best player, but I'm sure the fellows will soon learn my tricks.

Don't worry about me. I'm with good fellows who look after each other. Think of us and pray for our safety.

Love,
Sam"

After Jimmy read the letter aloud, Boone said, "That's the longest dang epistle I ever heared. Your teacher sure learned ya ta spin out a lot o' words. You could talk them Rebs inta surrender at this rate."

"D-D-Don't I-I-listen to him," replied the drummer boy. "T-T-That sounds r-r-real good except for the m-m-mother part. I always call her 'Ma'."

"Anything else? I'll be glad to rewrite it for you."

"Yeah. I d-d-didn't fight at D-D-Dranesville, so w-w-why talk about that? B-B-By the way, who w-w-was your drummer, then?"

"I was," said Jimmy, "until I proved myself a soldier in the battle."

"N-N-No f-f-foolin'?"

"I helped drive off the Rebels and captured two officers single-handed."

"I hate ta interrupt ya there, hero, but what's that word there?" asked Boone, pointing to the page.

"Confederates."

"Don't ya think ya should just call 'em Rebs?"

"Yeah," agreed Sam. "I think M-M-Ma would call 'em t-t-that, too. M-M-Ma don't use no f-f-fancy words. She g-g-gets to the p-p-point r-r-right quick."

"Okay, it's your letter."

While Jimmy changed the letter, a sullen, older private joined the group. He watched intently over Jimmy's shoulder, mouthing the words as they appeared on the paper.

"Boy, Lemon, I wish I could read as good as you," Boone said. "Why don't I ever see ya writin' letters ta home?"

Dan Lemon was a tall man with wind-burned, leathery skin. He had a bald spot on the top of his head and rarely was seen without his kepi cap, even indoors. He had an empty look about him that most men reserve for a loved one's funeral.

"I ain't got nobody at home," sighed the private.

"Nobody?"

"No. My wife run off with a slick-talkin' fella. I joined the army right after. You boys better watch out fer them women. Can't trust none of 'em."

"I . . . I . . . I'm sorry," stuttered Sam. "My pa run off an' I-I-left us, too. I . . . I . . . I'm g-g-glad he did . . . the way he b-b-beat M-M-Ma an' me."

"Well, I'm all done," said Jimmy, waving the paper in the air to dry the ink. "Now, all I need to do is get you an envelope and a stamp out of my haversack. Hey, have any of you boys seen my pack of stamps? Mother sent them when silver coins got scarce."

"When did you see 'em last?" asked Dan.

"Just yesterday I wrote a letter. I remember putting the stamps away before I went outside to watch Starr and Curtis fight."

"It looks like we got ourselves a sneak thief," Boone asserted. "I know that Bucky er Frank didn't take 'em. They's honest as the day is long."

"Oh, I wouldn't suspect them," replied Jimmy.

"An' Sergeant Curtis couldn'ta done it neither, 'cause he was too busy wrestlin' with Starr."

"S-S-Starr. I . . . I . . . I think that's yer m-m-man," suggested Sam.

"Why's that, Scarecrow?"

"Because I seen him creep back in here before a-a-anybody else. An' I . . . I . . . I jess d-d-don't I-I-like the I-I-looks o' him."

"Yes, but you can't accuse someone because you don't like his face," said Jimmy.

"Yeah, if bein' ugly made somebody a thief," joshed Boone, "all you boys would get con-victed."

"And didn't Starr's friend, Miles, come back in here with him? He had to have gone somewhere because he didn't hang around to cheer Lieutenant Colonel Kane."

"I think you're right, Jimmy. But don't worry. I'll keep my eyes an' ears open, an' we'll catch the rascal that made off with them stamps. He's bound ta make a mistake sooner er later."

"Thanks, Boone. I don't know what I'd do without friends like you and Bucky. Out of curiosity, why did you want to learn to read, anyway?"

"Well, heck. I can't play cards 'til I do. How's I supposed ta tell if I got a good hand if I can't tell a ten from a king? Besides, them fellas in Company C jess can't wait ta give away their pay."

"Why don't you just stick to checkers? You only need to know red from black to play that game."

"Ha. Ha. That's a real knee-slapper," grinned Boone.

"You're really not going to gamble if I teach you?" asked Jimmy with a frown.

"Why should that bother ya?" asked Lemon.

"Oh," said Scarecrow, "his father is a p-p-preacher."

"That don't hold no water with me. It's a travelin' preacher that stoled my wife."

Jimmy looked aghast at Dan Lemon while Boone's attention was drawn to the center of the tent. There Sergeant Curtis, Frank, and two privates began playing a boisterous game of euchre near the stove. It soon was evident that Curtis started winning by the way he whooped whenever he took a trick with an ace or a bower. Jeb Starr glared at the sergeant after each jubilant demonstration. Then the weasel-faced soldier muttered murderously to slack-jawed Private Miles, who nodded stupidly in agreement with every word.

Bucky sat away from the others near the tent mouth. He was fashioning a pipe from a root of mountain laurel, and he carved it with wondrous precision. On one side of the bowl he had inlaid a kepi cap decorated with a bucktail. On the other side he was carving a Springfield musket. He had almost finished the gun barrel when an orderly asked to be admitted.

Bucky untied the tent flap and held it open for the orderly. "Dang, it smells like a fox's den in here," griped the messenger, crossing the tent to warm his hands over the stove. "When's the last time you fellas bathed? I was supposed ta tell ya the supply wagons come this mornin'. You can fall out an' get yer rations. An' make sure ya ask fer some soap."

Although the storm had now abated and blown to the east, it left the camp buried in thigh-deep snow. The path to the quartermaster's shed had been obliterated except for the trail plowed by the orderly. Even following the orderly's tracks, it was tough going for Sergeant Curtis and the eleven men who trudged along behind him. It took them nearly twenty minutes to wade through the drifted snow that separated their tent from the supply shed.

"How did the wagons get through that blizzard?" wondered Jimmy aloud as he followed Curtis and Boone into the quartermaster's shed. "It's a miracle."

"They musta fitted the wagon teams with snowshoes," chuckled Boone.

"Maybe they come . . . before we really . . . got dumped on," puffed Corporal Comfort.

"I thought I heared 'em, but who could be sure with the sergeant yellin' 'bout the fire goin' out?" Lemon said.

Hosea Curtis only grunted and then went over to the quartermaster to collect his rations. The soldier whistled as he weighed out twelve ounces of bacon, one pound four ounces of fresh beef, one pound six ounces of soft bread, and one pound four ounces of cornmeal. While he portioned out the sergeant's beans, rice, coffee, sugar, soap, salt, potatoes, and molasses, Hosea asked, "Hey, ya got any more blankets? Mine caught fire last night when I bumped against the gol-dang stove."

"I think I kin fix ya up," said the quartermaster, handing Curtis half a blanket from a pile on the floor behind the counter.

"What's this? Why, this wouldn't even cover Starr's scrawny be-hind."

"Sorry, Sergeant, but we run low on blankets and had to cut 'em in half so everybody'd get one."

"This wouldn't even make my granny a decent shawl. Ain't there any full-sized ones?"

"Sorry. If ya don't want it, leave it fer someone smaller."

Grumbling, Curtis loaded his rations into his haversack and stuffed the half blanket on top. "Maybe I kin patch my burned one with this," he grunted. "Leave it ta the gol-dang army ta only stock blankets fit fer midgets."

Next, Boone moved forward to collect his provisions. Behind him, Jimmy, Bucky, Frank, Starr, and Corporal Comfort jostled for position.

"Bein' in the winter army ain't so bad after all," said Bucky. "There's always plenty o' food, and we don't even have ta hunt fer it."

"You're right," agreed Frank. "There's been plenty o' Januaries when I ain't had more than a few apples an' taters from the root cellar ta gnaw on."

"Last winter got so bad that even beaver tasted like a butterfly steak," sighed Bucky. "If Pa hadn't died, maybe things woulda been better."

"Boy, if I had to eat an old beaver, I'da joined up, too," said Corporal Comfort, eyeing the huge slab of bacon the clerk was slicing. "Is that why ya decided ta become a Bucktail?"

"No. It's 'cause Pa got killed by wolves."

"Oh!"

"Well, Bucky, all this good food seems to agree with you," said Jimmy. "Look at how you've filled out. I can't even see your ribs anymore."

"Yeah, Jimmy, I'm a sight bigger than my pa. I reckon I'll never outgrow his hawk nose, though."

After Bucky and his friends filled their haversacks, they trudged back to their tent and feasted on fresh beef and bread. They crowded around the stove to warm themselves and to savor the delicious smell of cooking meat.

Once they had their fill, Sergeant Curtis said, "We best feed up while we kin, boys. Once the fightin' starts again in the spring, we'll be back ta hardtack an' salt pork. By the way, I heared a funny song 'bout hardtack down at headquarters this mornin'. You boys wanna hear it? I asked an officer ta write down the words, so I wouldn't forgit none of 'em."

The soldiers cleared a space in front of the stove and drew their blankets into a semi-circle to watch the evening's entertainment. A hardtack box was used for a stage, and Hosea stepped up on it and bellowed:

Let us close our game of poker
Take our tin cups in our hand,
While we gather 'round the cook's tent door,
Where dry mummies of hard crackers
Are given to each man;
Oh, hard crackers, come again no more!

'Tis the song and sigh of the hungry
Hard crackers, hard crackers, come again no more!
Many days have you lingered upon our stomachs sore.
Oh, hard crackers, come again no more!

There's a hungry, thirsty soldier
Who wears his life away,
With torn clothes, whose better days are o'er,
He is sighing now for whiskey,

And, with throat as dry as hay,
Sings, hard crackers, come again no more!

'Tis the song that is uttered
By camp by night and day,
'Tis the wail that is mingled with each snore
'Tis the sighing of the soul
For spring chickens far away,
Oh, hard crackers, come again no more!

"Hey, Hosea," shouted Boone, "that was some song. But where's them spring chickens supposed ta come from?"

"From Virginy, o' course. The farms is said ta be loaded with fat hens ripe fer pluckin'. An' whiskey, too. I'd give a month's rations fer just a swig o' good corn liquor."

"Yeah, a little whiskey mighta helped ya sing in the right key!"

"Another thing I need ta find in Virginy is some good tobacco 'cause these half-an'-half ci-gars I been smokin' are lousy."

"W-W-What'd you m-m-mean, half-an'-half?" asked the drummer boy Scarecrow.

"Why, they's half horse crap an' half slivers."

After the laughter died down, Corporal Comfort came forward with his banjo and began plucking out the lively tune "Skip to My Lou." Dan Lemon accompanied him on the bones, and everyone began yelling for Scarecrow to do his clog dance. Shyly he refused until two men grabbed him by the arms and dragged him onto the hardtack box stage. He did a few clumsy steps until the jeers forced him to concentrate. Then he bit his lip and tapped out fancier moves that he had seen at a minstrel show. The soldiers cheered until their throats hurt and Scarecrow fell down exhausted.

Finally, Sergeant Curtis said, "Well, boys, there goes the bugler's extinguish lights call, so we best turn in. Remember the e-lection's tomorrow. They'll have it, snow or no snow. I don't know 'bout you, but I'm votin' fer Thomas Kane."

Everyone cheered at the mention of Kane's name except Jeb Starr and Private Miles, who sat muttering off by themselves. They continued to conspire even after the other soldiers snored in their blankets.

Bucktail reenactor Sharon Aaron, the camp cook, holds a basket of authentic hardtack. The hard biscuits are 3$\frac{1}{8}$ by 2$\frac{7}{8}$ inches in size and almost half an inch thick.

Chapter Three

GREEN SAUSAGE

Reveille blasted the soldiers out of their blankets on the morning of the election. Sergeant Curtis rose cursing from the cold ground and rousted his still half-asleep troops to the snowy parade ground for roll call. The men joined the rest of Company I of McKean County and snapped to attention when Captain Blanchard arrived from headquarters. The captain called out their names and jotted in a notebook those who were absent. Then, he, too, came to attention when Lieutenant Colonel Kane rode onto the field to inspect the regiment.

Kane, his dark eyes burning fiercely, sat erect on a dapple-gray horse that he directed with expert skill. As he rode to and fro among the ten companies, he surveyed rank after rank of hardened woodsmen, who had become crack shots in the mountains and forests of frontier Pennsylvania. These trappers, hunters, farmers, and lumbermen had come from Tioga, Perry, Cameron, Warren, Carbon, Elk, Chester, McKean, and Clearfield Counties, and Kane was proud of how they had jelled into a fierce fighting unit. Even standing in thigh-deep snow, they looked like a force to be reckoned with.

When Kane approached Company D of Warren County, he exchanged salutes with a tall captain, distinguished by a pointed nose and bushy, black beard. Hugh McNeil was his rival in the upcoming election for the colonelcy of the Bucktails, and Kane knew that the captain was a worthy opponent. McNeil had been a Yale man and a lawyer, and his education showed in his able handling of his company. He was also well liked for his pleasant personality. Even more important, in skirmish after skirmish, McNeil had demonstrated poise under fire, and his bearing exuded a confidence that the soldiers trusted.

After inspecting the men from Tioga, Carbon, Elk, and Chester Counties, Kane stopped to exchange words with his old friend, Captain Blanchard.

"How's everything going, Will?"

"Good, sir, except the recent inactivity has made the men pretty restless."

"I saw that the other night outside Curtis' tent. Why don't you have your company shovel the parade ground after breakfast, so we can get back to drilling this afternoon. That should cure what ails them."

"Yes, sir. Good luck in today's election."

Kane nodded to Blanchard and stared out at the rows of rugged men that comprised Company I. There was stout Sergeant Curtis, who once got busted to private for brawling and stealing timber. Then there was studious-looking Jimmy Jewett, one-time drummer and mama's boy. And, of course, how could he forget the orphan Indian, Bucky Culp? How far these men had come since signing the muster roll last April in Smethport. A smile flickered in Kane's beard as he thought about the undisciplined rascals and timid souls he had helped mold into fine soldiers. He had a special place in his heart for these men with whom he had shared so many dangers.

After the lieutenant colonel finished his inspection, he conferred with his captains to review the instructions for the day. Kane then rode off to headquarters, while the junior officers passed on the orders to the men. Hugh McNeil's

Warren County boys cheered the announced election as the two companies from Tioga County intermingled to discuss the merits of the two candidates for colonel.

Captain William Blanchard, meanwhile, told his soldiers: "Men, we were handpicked by Lieutenant Colonel Kane to clear off the parade ground after breakfast. When you're finished eating, report to the quartermaster's shed to pick up your shovels. This is important duty. If we don't drill, we'll get stale, and Johnny Reb will kick our be-hinds good for us. The colonel, excuse me, the lieutenant colonel, hopes to have the regiment out here this afternoon, so we best get rid of these drifts. After supper the election will be held, and I hope all of you will vote for the best man. That's all. Dismissed."

The men fell out of rank and trudged back to Bucktail City, slipping and sliding down the icy street. Sergeant Curtis noted with surprise that Jeb Starr never protested once after hearing about their extra duty. He joked with Miles, his slack-jawed friend, and even held open the tent flap for Culp, Comfort, Scarecrow, and Jewett before entering himself. Once inside, Starr further amazed his sergeant by offering to cook up a special breakfast for everyone.

"Now, why would you wanna go an' do that?" asked Curtis suspiciously.

"Yestiddy I traded my coffee ration to a farmer that comes into camp an' got some sassages," replied Starr. "I ain't been the most friendly fella lately, an' I jess wanna make it up ta everybody."

"No foolin'?" asked Frank.

"No foolin'."

Starr produced a huge ring of sausage from his haversack and began slicing it into an iron frying pan, which he took outside to heat over an open fire. The others followed him outside, and he whistled and exchanged pleasantries with Boone and Jimmy until Bucky said, "Hey, ain't that sassage kinda green?"

"That's jess the herbs an' spices them Dutch fellas puts in. That's what makes it so de-licious."

"Y-Y-Yeah," agreed Scarecrow. "They was j-j-jess this c-c-color back h-h-home on the f-f-farm."

The pungent aroma that wafted from the frying pork justified Scarecrow's words, and soon the entire troop was wolfing down thick slices of mouth-watering meat. It was so good that Boone was too busy stuffing his face to make wisecracks, and Comfort used both hands to devour his portion. Jimmy even forgot to say grace before tearing into the savory fare.

Only Bucky snuffed his plate like a dog and refused to eat. The rest of the men laughed when he warned, "All you fellas is gonna get mighty sick if ya gnaw this sassage. It's set too long to be any good."

"You're right," cackled Boone. "If it sets there on yer plate gettin' cold, it ain't gonna do nobody no good."

"How do ya know it ain't no good?" smirked Curtis. "Injun intuition?"

"Somethin' like that," replied Bucky, dumping his share of the sausage onto the open fire.

Sergeant Curtis, meanwhile, gobbled down seconds and thirds until the grease ran off his chin and down the front of his uniform. When he noticed that Starr and Miles had barely touched their food, he said, "If you boys ain't gonna eat that, why don't ya give it here?"

"Yes, sir, Sergeant," said Starr politely.

"I'm glad you're enjoyin' it," added Miles.

"Y-Y-Yeah," stuttered Scarecrow, "I . . . I . . . I ain't ever t-t-tasted nothin' this good. E-E-Even at h-h-home."

The men continued to gorge themselves until Curtis said, "Well, boys, I hate ta say it, but we best git over ta the parade ground before they come lookin' fer us."

"Yeah," agreed Frank, "if we eat much more, we'll be too stuffed ta work."

With reluctance, the soldiers set their tin plates in the tent and headed down the street with the rest of Company I. They found the going easier now because the other companies had already begun clearing paths and roadways in their sections of camp.

In front of the quartermaster's hut, Sergeant Curtis' men found Captain Blanchard directing two wagons onto the parade ground. Collecting shovels from a clerk, they began filling the wagons with heavy snow. It was backbreaking work even for former lumberjacks and dirt farmers.

Soon everyone but Bucky, Starr, and Starr's slack-jawed friend was sweating profusely and holding his cramping stomach. Curtis was the first to throw up, precipitating a volley of vomiting from the men in his squad. They made so much commotion that Blanchard came over to investigate.

"What's going on here?" blustered the captain. "Are you men so out of shape that you can't clear off a little snow without heaving? Or maybe you came by some corn squeezings. You should know by now that drinking is absolutely forbidden."

"W-W-We w-w-wasn't d-d-drinkin'," stuttered Scarecrow between retches. "I-I-It w-w-was the s-s-sassages. We all shoulda l-l-listened to B-B-Bucky."

"What sausages?"

Rising weakly from his knees, Sergeant Curtis said, "The ones Private Starr cooked up fer us this mornin'. He said he got 'em from the farmer that comes here regular when we gits our rations."

"Don't you men know better than to eat spoiled meat?"

"I didn't know it was bad," said Starr, feigning innocence. "Honest."

"Then, why didn't ya eat more of it?" growled Curtis.

"'Cause it was meant as a gift fer you boys. I didn't want ta be a hog."

"What a buncha manure. If I didn't feel so powerful bad, I'd cram my fist down yer throat an' let you chew on it fer awhile, you gol-dang snake."

"That's enough, Sergeant. Take your sick men back to camp. I'm sure I can find some other snow for you boys to move tomorrow. As of now, you're confined to quarters."

"But what about tonight's e-lection?"

"If you're too sick to work, you're too sick to vote."

"But, sir."

"Get along, Sergeant. You've held things up enough already. Lieutenant Colonel Kane expects this parade ground in marchable shape by this afternoon. Starr. Culp. Miles. Get back to work!"

As Curtis led his sick soldiers away, Bucky saw Jeb exchange knowing winks with slack-jawed Private Miles. He wanted to say something but knew it would only get him into trouble with Blanchard or some other officer. He didn't want to lose his vote, too, so he worked off his anger with his shovel.

The McKean Company filled twenty wagons with snow before the parade ground was ready for the afternoon drills. The exertion caused ten more exhausted men to fall out of rank. Even Bucky's arms felt like dead weight from four hours of shoveling wet snow that was heavy as mud. What kept him going was watching Starr grow paler with each shovelful he dug. It became apparent that he was lightheaded and nauseous, and Bucky kept hoping that the little weasel would vomit and get sent back to face Curtis' wrath.

When Lieutenant Colonel Kane arrived with the rest of the Bucktails, the McKean men formed into a sloppy rank and were given wooden rifles to drill with. This saved them from returning to their quarters to fetch their own Springfield muskets and holding up the other nine companies.

Bucky, Starr, and Miles stumbled half-dead through a jumble of drills that soldiers in the alert companies had trouble following. The lieutenant colonel barked out orders that were contradictory and had men marching into each other. Throughout the drills Kane appeared tense and unfocused. His horse whinnied and snorted as if sensing its rider's nervousness.

An hour of steady marching polished the parade ground into a skating rink. When Kane attempted to direct the McKean Company through a wheeling maneuver, Starr lost his footing and bowled over a whole row of troops. This sent a shiver of laughter through Company D of Warren County. Even Captain McNeil had trouble keeping a straight face. Luckily, there was no chance of discharging the wooden guns, and Kane canceled the drills before a mishap with real rifles might occur.

Afraid to return to their tent, Starr and Miles slunk off to see if they could bum supper from someone in another company. Bucky, though, was too queasy to eat. Rather than return to Bucktail City and disturb his sick friends, he wandered about Camp Pierpont to kill time before the election. First, he walked through the officers' quarter where the tents were built on log platforms to insulate them from the damp ground. Next, he inspected a row of Napoleon field pieces in the artillery park. Finally, he visited the stables and adjoining corral where the work horses and officers' mounts were penned.

While Bucky stroked the mane of a beautiful black mare, Starr and Miles strolled up the street and stopped to chat. Starr seemed genuinely proud of himself, the way he preened and patted his full belly. Miles, also, wore a gloating grin that Bucky wanted to punch off his face.

"How's it goin', Bucky?" asked Starr nonchalantly.

"Starr, that was a real mean trick ya pulled at breakfast."

"I don't know what you're talkin' about."

"I kin see why ya might take revenge on Sergeant Curtis. He ain't been real nice ta ya. But why poison them other men? It don't make no sense."

Instead of trying to defend his actions, Starr said, "After today's drillin' fi-asco, ain't ya ready ta vote fer McNeil?" "Hey, you kin go suck an egg. That's what weasels is best at. Even Colonel Kane kin have a bad day. I ain't turnin' my back on him jess 'cause you was clumsy an' fell down." "But what if I'da had a real gun an' it went off when I . . . slipped?" replied Starr with a smirk. "I'll bet I showed a lot o' fellows how unsafe it is ta follow Kane."

"Damn you," choked Bucky, his eyes widening with recognition. "I oughta drag ya back to our tent an' let ya explain all this to Hosea Curtis. I'm sure he'd be mighty interested."

While Bucky reached to grab Starr, Miles stuck out his leg and sent the Indian sprawling. Bucky slid under the corral rails on his face and suddenly found himself surrounded by agitated horses that snorted, fidgeted, and reared. He dared not move for fear of stampeding the herd and watched helplessly while Starr and Miles hightailed it back to the officers' quarter.

Bucky spoke softly to calm the horses and rose slowly to his feet. By the time he eased through the corral rails, a bugle was blowing assembly. He followed the sound back to the parade ground and rejoined the McKean Company. He wanted to tell Captain Blanchard about Starr, but he knew the damage had already been done.

After the ten companies of the Bucktail Regiment formed up and came to attention, Bucky saw Lieutenant Colonel Kane and Captain McNeil walk onto the field with General McCall and two of his staff officers. The latter disappeared into a hastily erected tent that would serve as the polling place. The voting was to be done by companies in alphabetical order, and each was summoned in turn.

Although the Bucktails voted on secret ballots, they made their choices very public when they emerged from the polling tent. It was evident to Bucky that the soldiers of Company A from Tioga County had split their votes by the way they argued while returning to their place on the parade ground. Company B from Perry County, on the other hand, was nearly unanimously in favor of McNeil. Cameron County's Company C shouted their support for Kane, while the Warren County boys hooted for their own captain when they left the polls. Company E, also from Tioga County, split their vote. Carbon County's Company F readily confessed to supporting McNeil. To Bucky it looked pretty hopeless for Kane until the Elk County boys of Company G and the lads of Chester County's Company H signaled in favor of the lieutenant colonel.

Finally, it was McKean County's turn to vote, and Bucky fidgeted and bit his lip with anticipation when a staff officer summoned them into the polling tent. Captain Blanchard stepped forward immediately and shouted, "Come on, men. Let's get in there and make our votes count for Colonel Kane." Half the company charged forward without hesitation, while a few other men looked around red-faced before going to vote for the hero they had followed from their wilderness homes into battle. Bucky went then, too, wishing Hosea and the other sick soldiers could have been there to help Kane.

When Bucky came out of the tent, he passed Starr entering with nearly a quarter of the McKean Company in tow. The weasel smiled in triumph and screeched, "Come along, boys. Let's push McNeil on to victory."

Bucky saw that it was now up to Company K of Clearfield County to determine the winner. They also must have realized it because it was awhile before anyone moved after a staff officer called their company. It took a second prompting before a stir ran through the ranks, and the soldiers moved forward to cast their votes for McNeil.

Although it was a frigid January evening, Bucky could feel the sweat run down his back while he waited for the results to be announced. Minutes seemed like hours, and the shadows lengthened ominously with the coming of night.

Finally, General McCall emerged from the polling tent, cleared his throat, and said, "Gentlemen of the Bucktail Regiment, you now have a new colonel. By 223 votes—Hugh McNeil has won the election. Colonel McNeil, will you please step forward."

McNeil marched smartly up to General McCall, saluted, and shook hands. Afterward, he received congratulations from Thomas Kane and a sword from the men of his old company. After Chaplain Hatton made the presentation, he prayed for the preservation and success of the Bucktail Regiment. Bucky had a hard time focusing on the words of the prayer when he thought about the votes for Lieutenant Colonel Kane that were lost to Starr's treachery.

Chapter Four

Run Rabbit Run

Starr and Miles shivered in the shadows outside their unit's tent until the extinguish lights bugle call sounded. With Sergeant Curtis' distinctive snoring muffling their entrance, they slunk through the tent flap and rolled themselves noiselessly in their blankets. Bucky, lying next to the entrance, saw them sneak in, but he did not let on that he was awake. He had purposely left the flap untied to see if they would have enough gall to return.

In the morning Starr and Miles were greeted with a reproachful silence by the rest of the squad. No one offered them hot coffee when it was ready, and Boone refrained from his usual jokes about their scrawny size. Sergeant Curtis did not harass them either or assign them any extra duties before he left for headquarters. Even Jimmy Jewett, the preacher's son, looked right through Starr when he said, "How ya doin' this mornin', fella?"

Starr could take a kick or an insult, but he couldn't stand to be ignored. When still no one had spoken to him by late afternoon, he sat down next to Bucky, who was putting the finishing touches on the pipe he was carving. Boone was standing next to the stove, and he edged closer to hear what Starr might say.

"That's a dandy pipe ya got there," Starr murmured with a sheepish grin. "How much ya want fer it?"

"Ain't fer sale."

"Maybe you'd be willin' ta trade it fer somethin' I picked up awhile back?"

"Ain't fer sale, Starr, whatever ya got."

"How 'bout postage stamps? Why, I got enough of 'em here ta last the whole war. With the shortage o' silver, an' all, they's as good as any coin."

"Come here, Jimmy," Boone said, sidling around the stove to nab Starr by the coat collar. "There's somethin' I want ya ta see."

Boone snatched the stamps from Starr's hand and gave them to Jimmy. "Do these look familiar?" he asked. "I think we jess nailed our sneak thief."

"What do ya mean by that?" protested Starr.

"Jeb, these stamps just didn't disappear from my haversack all by themselves. Why don't you explain how you happened to come by them?"

"Well, I . . ."

"That sure explains it fer me," growled Boone. "I think it's time we take a little walk over ta Captain Blanchard's tent."

"But—"

"Or would ya rather we de-liver ya directly ta the sergeant?"

"No."

"I don't think that'd be good neither," said Bucky. "Hosea might pound ya inta the ground like a tent peg."

"Yeah," agreed Boone. "Curtis is a friend o' ours, an' we don't wanna see 'im get in trouble over the likes o' you."

Bucky and Boone grabbed Starr and dragged him roughly up the street to headquarters where they found Sergeant Curtis muttering in heated tones to Captain Blanchard. While the captain listened to Curtis, thunderheads formed on his brow, and he spat tobacco disgustedly into a can next to his desk.

"Well, what do we have here?" Blanchard growled when Starr was thrust unceremoniously into the tent.

"Looks like a sassage-servin' weasel ta me, sir," said Curtis.

"Sergeant, after what you just told me about him trying to fix the election against Lieutenant Colonel Kane, it looks like a candidate for a week of midnight guard duty to me. Now, what sneaky trick did he pull, Crossmire?"

"Ask Private Jewett, sir. He'll be glad ta tell ya all about it."

"Well, Jewett?"

"My mother sent me some stamps last month, Captain, so I could write her regularly. The stamps got stolen from my haversack the night Lieutenant Colonel Kane returned to camp, and today Jeb Starr tried to trade them to Private Culp for a pipe he was whittling."

"I guess Private Starr needs *two* weeks of midnight guard duty to rehabilitate him."

"But ain't ya gonna listen ta my side o' the story?" muttered Starr.

"You mean, 'listen to my side of the story, sir'!" snapped Captain Blanchard. "And what exactly is that?"

"One night I found the stamps laying near the stove in our tent. I didn't know who they belonged to, so I picked 'em up. I meant ta find the owner. Honest, sir."

"Then, why did ya try tradin' 'em ta Culp?" barked Curtis.

"Hey, I know I put those stamps away the night they turned up missing," added Jimmy. "I always take care of my valuables. I never took them anywhere near the stove. I wouldn't want them to burn up."

"Um—"

"Now that I've heard Private Starr's brilliant defense," said Captain Blanchard evenly, "I think he needs to carry a haversack full of rocks while he's guarding the officers' latrine. Don't you agree, Sergeant Curtis?"

"Yes, sir."

"Of course, if Private Starr disagrees, he can always take his case to Lieutenant Colonel Kane. That's his right. Is that what you want, Private?"

"No, sir."

"Good. We'll see you back here tonight, Private Starr. Dismissed."

Flushing, Starr turned and strode from headquarters with Bucky, Boone, and Jimmy on his heels. When they were outside, Bucky said, "I think ya got off pretty easy, Jeb, considerin' all the dirt ya done around here lately."

"Yeah, Jeb, and you really disappointed me when you didn't admit to taking my stamps," sighed Jimmy. "But I forgive you like my father always says good Christians should."

"Yeah, but I don't," snapped Boone. "An' you kin bet I'll be watchin' ya from now on."

While Boone continued to hound Starr, Bucky said, "I'll see you fellas later. I got an errand ta run."

Bucky turned into the officers' quarter and walked along peering at the row of wall tents built on platforms. Before each one of them waved a banner, and Bucky continued on until he recognized the tattered Bucktail standard he had followed in battle. Here, he paused to call through the tent flap, "Lieutenant Colonel Kane, sir. It's me, Private Bucky Culp, askin' permission ta enter, sir."

"Come in, Private Culp."

When Bucky entered Kane's quarters, he found the lieutenant colonel busy writing at a collapsible camp table set up in the far corner. The officer's face wore a pensive look, and his foot tapped nervously on the board floor.

"I'm sorry ta disturb ya, sir, but I jess finished carvin' this here pipe an' I thought ya might like it. I know it ain't as good a gift as a sword or anything, but it took a long time fer me ta finish it."

Kane took the pipe Bucky offered and admired the Bucktail cap and musket that were beautifully inlaid on the sides of the bowl. The craftsmanship was intricate and unique, and the lieutenant colonel said in an awed voice, "Why, thank you, Private Culp. I don't think I've ever seen such a finely carved pipe."

"I'm glad ya like it, sir," said Bucky humbly. "Sir, I . . . I . . . I'm sure sorry 'bout the way the e-lection turned out. I wanted ya to know that I voted fer ya like I promised."

"Your loyalty could never be questioned, Private, and I'm proud to have had the opportunity to lead fine soldiers like you. I'll always remember the courage you and the other brave lads displayed at Dranesville. If you'll excuse me now, I have to get back to work. Thanks again for your gift. It's too finely crafted to tarnish with tobacco smoke, but it will make a wonderful memento of my days with the Bucktails."

As Bucky saluted and turned to leave, Captain Blanchard called through the tent flap, asking permission to enter. Bucky saluted the captain on the way out and then loitered outside to see if Starr would get in more trouble.

"What's the matter, Will?" asked Kane. "The way your jaw is working, you look like you're really angry."

"You're darn right I'm angry, sir. Sergeant Curtis just told me how Private Jeb Starr tried to sabotage the election, and it really burns my bacon. Who knows how many votes that weasel might have cost you. I think we should take this information to General McCall and demand a new election."

"Will, I don't want to hear it. Hugh McNeil is colonel now, and the last thing he needs is controversy. I know Hugh will do a good job with the regiment because he's a brave and dedicated officer. Your men are to refrain from all demonstrations of discontent."

"Yes, sir."

"Above all, they should not remove their bucktails from their caps nor bury them. The bucktail is a symbol of our regiment's unity. It identifies us as woodsmen and sharpshooters. It should be displayed no matter who's in command."

"So, you're not disappointed that you didn't get elected?"

"I was until I realized that I have an even bigger contribution to make. Now I'll have more time to work on this paper I'm writing."

"Paper, sir?"

"I call it 'Instructions for Skirmishers.' It details a set of tactics I've devised for the deployment of riflemen. In a way the paper is a protest against ineffective European tactics being forced on the men of the Union army."

"Sounds interesting, sir."

"I hope General McClellan thinks so because I plan to submit my paper to him when it's finished."

"What's the gist of your new tactics? If you care to say, sir."

"I do care to say," Kane laughed. "After leading soldiers like those under your command, I truly believe that handpicked riflemen can be used in the same manner as cavalry. If the Bucktails traveled without tents and heavy provisions, they could match horsemen in speed, stamina, and effectiveness. Our woodsmen should have no problem being without rations for a few days, or even weeks, because they're used to living off the land. I just hope I get the chance to prove my theories, Will."

"I hope so, too, sir. For now, though, I better get back to Bucktail City. It soon will be time to assemble the men. I'll be sure to inform them that they are not to demonstrate against the election results."

Beaming at the words he had just overheard, Bucky slipped behind an adjacent tent when Blanchard came out onto the path. After the captain disappeared from view, Bucky left officers' row and crossed the parade ground. Kane's tactics still ran through his head when he entered the street leading to Bucktail City. He could hardly wait to share the news.

When Bucky ducked into his quarters, Starr and Miles were nowhere to be seen. The rest of the men were gathered around the stove discussing Starr's punishment.

"I think they shoulda drummed Jeb outta the army fer what he done," suggested Corporal Comfort.

"That'd be too good fer him," said taciturn Dan Lemon. "They should shoot the thievin' skunk."

"O-O-Or t-t-tar an' f-f-feather h-h-him," added Scarecrow. "What do you t-t-think, B-B-Bucky?"

"I think ya should listen ta what I overheared Lieutenant Colonel Kane tell Captain Blanchard."

"Ya better watch that eavesdroppin'," laughed Boone. "Some might take that fer spyin'."

"Shut up, Boone," growled Sergeant Curtis. "Come on, Bucky, what did ya hear?"

"Why, the lieutenant colonel has come up with some new tactics that'd make us into light-travelin' scouts, an' we'd be used like cavalry. Wouldn't it be great not ta be slowed down by a bunch o' rations an' equipment?"

"But what would we eat?" asked Corporal Comfort, hugging his pudgy stomach.

"Gol-dang it. Whatever we could find," snapped Curtis.

"A-A-An' w-w-where w-w-would we s-s-sleep?" wondered Scarecrow.

"On the gol-dang ground as usual, you sissy."

"Maybe it's the Indian in me talkin'," added Bucky, "but I'd like nothin' better than ta return ta the old ways o' livin' off the land."

"Jess so them old ways don't lead ya ta scalpin' Rebs," growled Curtis.

"You know me better than that, Sergeant. I'm really sorry yer folks was killed by my people years ago. An' I understand why it took so long fer ya ta accept me. All I meant was that I miss marchin' through the woods an' chasin' Rebs. I'm so sick o' rottin' in this here camp. I can't wait fer spring."

"I'm with ya, Bucky," agreed Boone. "I've been restless as a porcupine trapped in an outhouse. Let's get on with this here fight."

"Me, too," said Frank Crandall. "An' I like Lieutenant Colonel Kane's new tactics. Maybe if we moved fast an' struck them Rebs where they least expected, we'd win this war an' get back home once an' fer all."

"Heck, I'd jess be happy ta get outta this stinkin' tent fer awhile," grumbled Curtis. "Anybody wanna take a walk before Camp Pierpont turns back into a gol-dang mud hole?"

Curtis ducked through the tent flap, followed by the rest of his squad. The sun had peeked through the clouds, and puddles of melted snow already dotted the street.

The soldiers meandered along dejectedly past the boundaries of the encampment until Boone said, "Hold up there, boys. Look over yonder by that stump. Is that what I think it is? Is anybody ready fer a game o' run rabbit run? Remember now. Only bare hands is allowed."

Sure enough, the sun had beckoned a young rabbit from its burrow, and the Bucktails moved stealthily to surround it before it could bolt. They inched into a crude circle, and when the rabbit ran, Bucky jumped in front of it to herd it toward Jimmy. Jimmy grabbed for it, missed clumsily, and chased it toward Frank. Frank had no better luck catching it but kept it inside the circle where it ran toward Comfort. When the corporal lunged forward, he fell on his fat belly. Next, the rabbit evaded Scarecrow. Only Boone separated the swift creature from freedom, and the lanky woodsman snared it by the scruff of the neck just as it broke for the latrine.

"Boy, he's gonna make a fine stew," said Comfort, licking his lips. "That little fella should be nice an' tender."

"No. No," replied Boone, releasing the scared rabbit. "You know the rules. We always let 'em go in case they wanna play some other time. If only Stonewall Jackson was this easy ta catch, we'd be all set."

Chapter Five

Wood Foraging

The next morning the sun rose, the temperature soared, and the mud was ankle-deep by noon. Again all drilling was suspended, and Bucky became so bored that he volunteered to go on the wood-foraging expedition organized by Sergeant Curtis. Surprisingly, Jeb Starr and Miles also asked to go along. The rest of the party included Boone and Frank.

"Why has firewood become so scarce?" asked Bucky as they left Bucktail City and went to requisition a wagon and two draft horses from the camp stable.

"It's the gol-dang government that keeps us scroungin' fer wood," explained Curtis. "They never send us enough fer the whole camp. 'Course the Rebs already come through and burned all the fence rails. What's left is a few windfalls an' that green stuff we usually fill our stove with."

"Well, Sergeant," joked Boone, "maybe today we oughta jess keep goin' 'til we finds us some nice oak an' maple ta burn. There's plenty o' that grows up yonder in McKean County."

The men rode through the muddy countryside for what Bucky guessed to be over five miles before they came to a woodlot that hadn't been raided by the Rebs or the soldiers of Camp Pierpont. There they found some mature birch and fell to notching the trees with double-bladed axes.

Bucky noticed that Jeb Starr seemed especially driven in his attempt to fell a good-sized tree. He hacked frantically, spraying bark and wood chips in all directions for a good ten minutes until the tree tottered. Then Starr waited until Sergeant Curtis came down the path dragging a dead log. At the exact moment Hosea passed beneath Starr's tree, the wiry man struck his ax into the weak spot on the trunk and sent it crashing to the ground. The birch missed Hosea's head by inches and blew him forward.

"Gol-dang you, Starr," howled Curtis when he saw who had felled the tree. "Now you're gonna pay."

Hosea rushed Starr, wrenched the small man's ax from him, and flung it into the brush. Starr tried to wiggle free but slipped in the red mud, pulling the sergeant down on top of him. Hosea flailed his enemy with his fists until Starr's face swelled up as if he'd been stung by a nest of paper wasps. Before Bucky and Frank could pull their sergeant off, Jeb's eyes wore raccoon circles and blood flowed from a nasty gash on his chin.

Miles tried several times to come to his friend's aid, but Hosea batted him away with his huge paws. When Curtis was back on his feet, he flung off Bucky and Frank and headbutted Miles until blood gushed from the little fellow's smashed nose. This time it took Bucky, Frank, and Boone to restrain their blood-crazed sergeant.

After his attacker had been dragged a safe distance away, Miles threatened, "Curtis, this time you've gone too far."

"That's *Sergeant* Curtis ta you, Private."

"Well, Sergeant Curtis, when we git back ta camp, me an' Starr here are gonna see about gettin' ya court-martialed."

"Not if we bury ya out here, an' say ya was captured by Rebs."

"Ya wouldn't dare do that," said Miles smugly, but his eyes told another story.

"Yes, we would," snarled Frank, with Bucky and Boone nodding in agreement. "We're all sick of yer vicious schemes. First, ya work ta defeat Kane in the e-lection, an' now ya almost smash Hosea ta jam. I'd rather be bunkin' with a wolverine than with the two o' you."

Miles helped up Starr, and they staggered off, bleeding, in the direction of Camp Pierpont. When they disappeared into the brush, Bucky asked, "Do ya think either of 'em will squeal?"

"Nah, they ain't got the guts," assured Hosea. "If you boys hadn't pulled me off, I'da fixed their wagons once an' fer all."

"Come on," said Frank. "Let's get back ta work. We gotta gather us some wood, or we'll be mighty cold tonight when the sun goes down."

Bucky and Boone picked up their axes and returned to felling trees that Frank trimmed of branches and hacked into manageable lengths. Hosea, still quivering with anger, manhandled Frank's logs onto the bed of the wagon.

It was mid-afternoon before the soldiers started the long trek back to camp. It started to rain again, and the men sloshed along cursing beside the creaking wagon driven by their sergeant. Often the wagon bogged down in the mud and had to be unloaded to break it free. By the time camp was reached, Bucky and the others were exhausted, drenched, and totally famished.

While the soldiers unloaded the firewood near their tent, they shouted for their neighbors to come help themselves. Bucky, Frank, and Boone gathered up armfuls of wood and went inside to get warm. The sergeant, however, had to return the wagon to the stable, and his men could hear him cursing until he was well out of sight.

When Bucky entered the Sibley tent, he found four members of his squad inside. Jimmy and Scarecrow were busy playing checkers while the two recruits were huddled together reading letters and swapping news from home.

"Why didn't any of you fellas come out an' help us unload the wagon?" asked Frank, piling his load of wood by the stove.

"Sorry," replied Jimmy, "I guess we were so engrossed in our game that we didn't think of it."

"Well, maybe we'll be too engroused in sleepin' er eatin' next time we run outta wood," said Boone, rubbing his sore biceps. "Then, it'll be up to yer lordships ta git it."

"I said I was sorry," snapped Jimmy, stung by Boone's comment.

"Any o' you fellas seen Starr an' Miles?" asked Bucky matter-of-factly while he warmed his hands over the stove.

"Yeah, they come in all busted up," said one of the recruits. "Said they was in some kinda accident."

"They gathered up their bedrolls and went over to the hospital," added Jimmy. "By the looks of their faces, that must have been some accident."

"Yeah, they accidentally fell against the sergeant's fists," chortled Boone. "Didn't they tell ya what happened?"

"N-N-No," stammered Scarecrow. "A-A-All they said was that they w-w-wanted to f-f-find some new b-b-bunkmates an' to n-n-not expect them b-b-back."

"What really happened out there?" asked Jimmy.

"Just like they said," replied Frank, after directing a warning glare at Boone. "They was hurt in a foragin' accident."

Bucky sat down with Jimmy and Scarecrow. The drummer said, "G-G-Guess what, B-B-Bucky. J-J-Jimmy asked his folks to look in on my m-m-ma, an' n-n-now she's s-s-stayin' in S-S-Smethport with them."

"Yeah, I received a letter from Mother today. Do you want me to read it to you, Bucky?"

"Sure. How is yer ma doin'? She's a mighty fine lady. I hope you've been tellin' her 'hello' fer me from time ta time."

"Mother's doing fine. You never have to worry about her forgetting you, Bucky."

"That's good, 'cause I'm gonna start sendin' her my pay ta keep fer me 'til after the war."

"W-W-Why do you w-w-want to do that?" asked Scarecrow.

"I'll need money fer supplies if I wanna return ta trappin'. A lot o' Pa's traps was old, an' I'll need gunpowder an' clothes an' lots o' other stuff."

"That's really using your head, Bucky," agreed Jimmy. "I'll tell Mother about your plan the next time I write. Are you ready to hear her letter now?"

"Yeah, go ahead."

15 January 1862
Smethport, Pennsylvania

My Dear Jimmy,

How is everything at Camp Pierpont? I'm glad that your winter has been mild, even though the warmer temperatures have caused the mud you keep complaining about. The canceled drills are actually a good thing because now you boys can catch up on the rest you all need so badly after all the marching you did last year.

How is Bucky doing? Your father and I are both so thankful you have him. I know that you are now a full private, too, but it never hurts to have a wonderful friend like Bucky to lend you a helping hand.

Father visited Sam's mother like you asked, and he found her in deplorable condition, with little food or firewood. We thought it best if she came and lived with us until Sam returns with you. She is now comfortably settled into your old bedroom. She is such a sweet lady and is so thankful for our company. I pray daily that this cruel war gets over soon and that you, Sam, and Bucky are safe.

Love,
Mother

"W-W-What does 'de-plor-able' m-m-mean?" asked Scarecrow when Jimmy had finished.

"It means your mother was in pretty bad shape."

"Yeah, but she ain't n-n-now, thanks to your m-m-ma and p-p-pa."

"You best believe it," agreed Bucky. "Sam, you oughta see their fine house in Smethport. It's got two stories an' everything."

"N-N-No f-f-foolin'?"

"Yeah, an' Jimmy's ma is the kindest lady I ever met. An' can she cook. I stayed with the Jewetts before Jimmy an' me enlisted, an' she whipped me up the best breakfast I ever ate."

"H-H-How can I ever t-t-thank you, J-J-Jimmy? You gotta be the b-b-best friend a fella ever had for h-h-helpin' my m-m-ma like ya done."

"It was the Christian thing to do, Sam. Hey, do you want to go outside and practice those drum rolls I showed you?"

"S-S-Sure thing. You can come too, B-B-Bucky."

"No thanks, Sam. I think I'm jess gonna crawl in my bedroll an' rest after all the woodcuttin' I done today. I must be gettin' soft like the sergeant said. You fellas go ahead."

"We also got some more good news today," added Jimmy. "It seems that Kane's skirmish tactics were accepted by General McClellan. All of us McKean boys, along with Companies C, G, and H, got assigned to train with the lieutenant colonel. That means we'll get to follow our favorite officer."

"I'll bet Starr an' Miles will love that," said Frank with a wry smile.

"If I was you boys, I wouldn't get too comfortable," boomed Sergeant Curtis, pushing his big frame through the tent flap.

"Why not?" asked Boone. "We sure earned us some rest after all the wood we lugged today."

"Kane's orderly caught me on the way back from the stables an' said that the lieutenant colonel wants ta see us wood foragers down at his tent."

"Sounds like Starr's gonna make trouble after all," said Frank.

"We'll learn soon enough," grunted Curtis.

The sergeant, Bucky, Frank, and Boone splashed glumly through the muddy streets of Bucktail City, across the parade ground, and into the officers' quarter. Nobody spoke until they arrived at Kane's tent, where Curtis asked and received permission to enter. Inside the tent they found the heavily bandaged Starr and Miles already there. Starr's eyes were practically swollen shut, and Miles' broken nose jutted at a crazy angle. Both soldiers stood humbly with their heads bowed and their hats in their hands before the seated lieutenant colonel.

The sergeant and his men saluted Kane. After an awkward silence, Curtis asked, "Do you want ta see us, sir?"

"Sergeant Curtis, Privates Starr and Miles have just made some serious accusations against you, but I wanted to hear your side of the story before I decide what should be done."

"Sir, I'd like ta hear what I'm being accused of be-fore I say anything."

"Very well, Sergeant. That seems fair enough. I'll ask Private Starr to repeat what he told me. Private—."

"Like I said before, Lieutenant Colonel Kane, sir, me an' Miles have been in the sergeant's doghouse fer some time. We thought maybe we could right that situation by takin' on some extra duty. Sorta clean the slate."

"So you volunteered to go on the foraging party?" asked Kane.

"Yes. You know. Gatherin' wood fer the company."

"After that what happened?"

"Well, sir, I takes on this big birch that was close ta the road an' easy ta haul an' load. Jess as I was ready ta lay the tree down, a wind come up an' blew it over before I intended. Before I could say how sorry I was, the sergeant there went crazy an' started pummelin' me. He claimed I done it on purpose. Truth be told, I never felled that tree. The wind done it. I'd never bushwhack a fella. That's the plain truth."

"Private Starr, you said the sergeant pummeled you," repeated Kane. "What injuries did you receive?"

"As you kin see, sir, my whole face got busted up good. An' then I got cuts on both arms, an' a busted rib er two."

"Sir, he's a gol-dang liar," exploded Curtis, striding menacingly toward Starr. "That faker's got bandages on places there ain't no cuts. If I really meant ta hurt that weasel, he'da not returned at—"

"Yes, sir, an' that reminds me," shot back Starr. "The sergeant an' them other fellas threatened ta bury me an' Miles out in the woods ta keep us from talkin'."

"Why you. I oughtta tear yer—"

"Sergeant, that's enough," barked Kane. "Order or I'll get some sentries in here. Order!"

Boone and Frank grabbed Curtis and pulled him away from Starr before the sergeant did anything to add to the charges against him. "Calm down," whispered Boone. "You're doin' 'xactly what Starr wants."

"Private Miles," said Kane, "can you confirm what Private Starr just said about the sergeant?"

"Yes, sir. He was mad enough ta kill us, too. If ya ask me, he overreacted when the tree fell next ta him. It wouldn'ta come that close if he'da jumped right away. It seemed like he wanted ta be hit, so he'd have an excuse ta attack Jeb."

"You're a lyin' weasel," erupted Curtis. "Starr waited 'til I was right under that tree be-fore he dropped it. He's been lookin' fer a chance ta git me, an' he took it."

"That's the way it looked ta me, too, sir," said Bucky, stepping between Curtis and Starr. "I was restin' fer a minute an' seen the whole thing. Sure as I'm standin' here, Starr tried ta squish the sergeant an' then got the beatin' he deserved."

"Private Culp, that's for me to decide," howled Kane. "I think you men are too full of fight for your own good. I know just the thing to cure that. For the next week you will be placed on half rations. In addition, Starr and Miles will be confined to the hospital. Tomorrow the rest of you hooligans will march in a circle around Camp Pierpont from sunup until lights out is sounded. If you drop out of line, you will repeat the exercise the next day. And the next. Until you get it right. Understood?"

"Yes, sir," said the soldiers, cowed by their commander's sudden outburst.

"By rights, I should have the whole lot of you court-martialed," continued Kane with a growl. "If I hear even another whisper of this feud, you'll feel the full force of my wrath."

"Yes, sir."

"Oh, Curtis, Culp, Crossmire, Crandall. Report back here at first light."

"Yes, sir."

"Starr. Miles."

"Yes, Lieutenant Colonel?"

"Report to the hospital. And remove those phony bandages. Next week you two fakers will serve the same sentence as the others. Dismissed! All of you!"

Chapter Six

BUCKY'S RESTLESSNESS

Bucky's restlessness at Camp Pierpont reached a peak during late February and early March. Training remained suspended due to the ankle-deep mud that even made trips to the latrine difficult. Then news of Union victories in the West at Fort Henry and Fort Donelson by a General Grant swept through Bucktail City, making Bucky itchier yet for action.

What made Bucky most discontented, though, was Jimmy's growing friendship with Scarecrow. The two had become inseparable since Scarecrow's ma had moved in with the Jewetts, and Jimmy began treating Sam like his little brother. If Jimmy wasn't writing letters for Sam, he was showing him new drum rolls or teaching him to read. They actually seemed happy to be cooped up in the tent day after day.

One morning Bucky sat next to Jimmy and Scarecrow to watch their game of checkers. When they were a move or two from finishing, Bucky asked, "Do you fellas mind if I play, too?"

"Why don't you see if Boone will play you?" replied Jimmy. "Checkers is a two-man game, and I already have Sam as my opponent."

"Well, what if I take on the winner?"

"Sorry, we have to leave right after this game."

"Y-Y-Yeah," added Sam. "We're gonna m-m-mail s-s-some letters down at h-h-headquarters."

Downhearted, Bucky rose without another word, grabbed his rifle and haversack, and strode toward the tent flap. Sergeant Curtis was playing cards with Frank, Dan Lemon, and Corporal Comfort, and he grunted as Bucky passed, "Where are ya goin', Culp?"

"I'm bored, Sergeant. I'm gonna git me a little air."

"What do ya need yer gun fer?" asked Boone from where he was warming himself by the stove. "Air don't need killed before ya kin breathe it."

"I . . . I . . . I need some target practice."

"I think he's plannin' ta desert," said Frank with a wink. "How 'bout you, Sergeant?"

"Hey, if Culp says he's goin' shootin', that's where he's goin'. How kin I pick on the fella after the way he stood up fer me in that hearin' with Kane? If it weren't fer Bucky comin' ta my de-fense, I'da slugged Starr an' would be bustin' rocks in some army prison. I say Culp is a dang good fella, even if he is an Injun."

"Hey, while you're out, Bucky, why don't ya look fer Starr an' Miles?" asked Dan Lemon. "None of us has been able ta find out where they's bunkin'."

"I heared Kane took 'em in," snickered Corporal Comfort.

"An' I heared they live in the cellar of the officers' outhouse," chortled Boone.

"If it was me, I'd look down at the camp dump for 'em," added Frank. "That's where the rest of the local skunks kin be found."

"Jess be back before dinner, Bucky," ordered the sergeant. "Remember, it's yer turn ta cook tonight."

Bucky slid through the tent flap and sloshed up the main street of Bucktail City toward the outskirts of camp. He was very familiar with Pierpont's perimeter after carrying out Lieutenant Colonel Kane's punishment. He also was on speaking terms with all the sentries from his many laps around the camp. When Bucky reached the guard post, he wasn't even questioned by the sergeant in charge. The soldier just waved and said with a laugh, "I see you're bein' punished again. Good luck, fella."

Bucky saluted in response and slopped off down the road into the Virginia countryside. He hiked steadily for an hour until he came to a thick grove of pines that he figured was out of gunshot range of the camp. There he loaded his rifle and began blasting one pine cone after another from the highest branches of the tallest tree.

After twenty minutes of shooting and reloading, Bucky grew weary of target practice and scouted the brush for a fresh game trail. He didn't have to hunt long before he found where rabbits ran with regularity through a prickly hedge. After fashioning a snare from a piece of rope he fetched from his haversack, he sat with his back against a tree to wait for his lunch to come hopping up the trail.

Bucky closed his eyes and fell into a fitful slumber. In his dreams he ran around and around Camp Pierpont, chased by a horde of Rebels with the faces of wolves. His pa, Iroquois, was running with him, but the faster they sprinted, the closer the Rebs got. Bucky could actually feel their wolf breath on his back when he was jarred awake by the snap of the triggered snare.

Bucky's hands trembled while he cleaned the dead rabbit. As he moved about gathering deadfalls for his cooking fire, he thought: This soldier's life is really gettin' ta me. Why should I go back at all when I could head north an' return ta the ways o' my people? The fightin' will never end anyhow. Once the Rebs is beat, we'll still have the Starrs ta deal with. Jimmy don't need me no more, so what's the point o' stayin'? Livin' alone in the forest is best.

Starting the fire with little pine twigs, Bucky added bigger branches until the flames licked merrily upward. The Indian lad threaded the rabbit on a spit and turned it slowly over the fire, savoring the delicious aroma of roasted, fresh-killed flesh. Then he made the mistake of staring into the flames where images of Iroquois attacked by a bear, Iroquois drunk and bleeding, and Iroquois ripped by wolves danced in the shimmering light. But the tears didn't come until Bucky gnawed listlessly on the roast rabbit that should have been a real treat after months of army rations. He knew he must return to Boone, Frank, and the other grinning faces waiting for him back at camp. To choose the living over the dead was really the only choice.

Bucky trudged up the road to Camp Pierpont in the growing gloom of evening and saluted another chuckling guard who heckled, "Back from yer punishment walk already? I'm gonna have ta have a talk with that Lieutenant Colonel Kane fer lettin' ya off so easy."

"Hopefully, I'm outta the woods now," replied Bucky with a sad smile.

Instead of returning directly to his tent to cook supper like he was ordered, Bucky wandered aimlessly about Pierpont for the next hour, ending up at the camp stables. He circled around to the corral and leaned against the rails, dejectedly pondering his future. Thoughts of desertion again flickered through his mind until a soft-muzzled mare trotted over to nuzzle against his arm. While Bucky stroked the mare's nose and mane, he realized the futility of running away. The mud would be his enemy there, too, for he could not expect to walk very far before he was missed. He wouldn't be able to hide his tracks, either, and stealing a horse was not an option. He would never do anything to disgrace his dead pa, Iroquois. He broke into a sweat thinking about how foolish he had been to risk leaving camp at all.

The sky dimmed, and dusk crept across the parade ground and into the corral. Bucky knew he should get back and start supper, but somehow he couldn't leave the newfound friend that snuggled against him. For the most part, his life had been devoid of affection. His mother had died when he was a tad, and his pa was never generous with his praise or love. Finally, Bucky vented his frustration by wondering aloud, "Why did Jimmy go an' shut me out? Why did he shut me out?"

At the last glimmer of twilight, Bucky heard the splash of boots coming around the stable. The other time he had come here, he had run into Starr and Miles. Bucky tensed at the thought and tried to hide. Before he could duck behind a fence post, two shadows appeared in the half-light and hurried toward him. He closed his hands into fists as one of the shadows flashed out his right arm. Instead of the anticipated blow, Bucky felt a playful hand slap him on the shoulder.

"There you are," said Frank with relief. "The sergeant sent me an' Boone out lookin' fer ya when ya didn't come back before supper."

"Yeah," added Boone. "Hosea was jumpier than a cat on a hot griddle, so we best hightail it back. He'll probably chew ya out good, Bucky, but that's jess 'cause he's worried about ya."

"That goes fer me, too," said Frank. "What's been eatin' ya lately, anyhow?"

"It's this here mud. It's gettin' ta me bad. It's even worse than deep snow. I feel like a beaver caught in a steel trap. But I can't escape even if I did gnaw off my own leg."

"Why didn't ya tell us instead o' goin' off like ya did?" asked Boone. "After we tramped halfway across Pennsylvany, rafted down a ragin' river, an' dodged Reb Minie balls together . . . why . . . you're jess as good as my brother."

"Yes sir-ee," agreed Frank, slapping Bucky on the back. "You're better than my brother. He was too dang busy gettin' hitched ta some floozy he met in a pig's ear ta come off ta war with me."

Bucky grinned broadly in the dark and followed his friends back to Bucktail City. The mud sucked at their boots every step of the way, and several times Frank, who was in the lead, tripped in sink holes and fell headlong on the sloppy street. Sentries harassed them, too, about being away from their quarters after dark. Each time, Boone got by these guards by saying, "Our unit's fairly crawlin' with cooties, an' our stinkin' sergeant sent us fer some special soap. Come on over here an' stick yer fingers in my hair. You'll see soon enough I ain't lyin'."

It was well over an hour before Bucky and his friends arrived back at their tent. Expecting a good tongue lashing, Bucky entered last and went and sat quietly on his blanket.

"It's about gol-dang time you boys got back," growled Sergeant Curtis from where he hovered next to the stove. "Get yer be-hind over here, Bucky, an' have some beef we saved fer ya. I was gonna assign ya cookin' duty fer the next week, but ya lucked out."

"How's that, Sergeant?"

"Word come from headquarters that we's movin' out o' Camp Pierpont tomorrow. We's each ta git one hundred rounds o' catridges an' three-days cooked rations in the mornin'. That's all. We ain't luggin' no tents with us."

"Where do ya think we's headin'?" asked Frank.

"I heared from the boys in Captain McDonald's company that General McClellan has come up with a new plan o' attack. Accordin' ta those fellas, Little Mac is gonna ship the whole gol-dang army ta the Virginy Peninsula an' hit Richmond from the east."

"Why don't he jess push south from Manassas like be-fore?"

"Well, Frank, there's too many rivers an' swamps ta cross, an' the gol-dang Rebs is more plentiful than mosquitoes."

"Sergeant, what's tomorrow's date?" asked Jimmy, looking up from the Bible passage he was reading Sam. "I'd like to know, so I can tell the folks back home when we left winter camp."

"The tenth o' March. That's the date they wrote on them dispatches I seen down at headquarters."

"Let's go out an' shoot off some guns, er somethin'," said Frank. "If we actually do leave this miserable camp tomorrow, it's gonna seem like the Fourth o' Ju-ly."

Chapter Seven

BREAKING CAMP

It took all the next morning for the quartermaster corps to issue rations and ammunition to the soldiers of Camp Pierpont, so the Bucktails weren't assembled into marching formation until noon. Bucky jammed into line next to Jimmy and fidgeted restlessly until Sergeant Curtis called the men to attention. Boone and Frank continued to grin even then while Dan Lemon and Corporal Comfort were glumly silent. The two recruits stood stiffly in rank, their eyes flashing with trepidation. Sensing their anxiety, Bucky was thankful that he had already experienced the roar and chaos of battle. While these violent images played in his head, he saw Starr and Miles steal silently into the line next to Comfort.

Sam, his hat slipping down over his ears, rushed to join a covey of drummers who started a long roll beat that set the division into motion. The camp-weary men burst into a chorus of cheers that even the overcast skies could not dampen. The road was still sloppy with red mud, and the splash of marching feet reminded Bucky of the slap of a beaver's tail that warned its kind of danger.

After the soldiers warmed to the pace of the march, Bucky said to Jimmy, "Yer friend Scarecrow sure has improved his drummin' since ya started workin' with 'im."

"I think he's doing a lot better, too. If he keeps working as hard as he has, he'll be a private like us in no time."

"I saw you learnin' him readin' an' letter writin'. You must be a good teacher."

"Well, thank you, Bucky. I'd teach you if you'd let me. I'm sorry I didn't spend much time with you in camp. Sam just needed so much help with everything that I kinda lost track of everybody else. Teaching Sam was my way of dealing with that dreadful, boring winter."

"Does that mean we're still friends?"

"Of course we are, Bucky. I don't think I'd have made it through the first year of war . . . without you."

"Hey, I hate ta break up such a heartwarmin' conversation," chuckled Boone from the next row of marchers, "but don't you boys think it's kinda strange that we're goin' back towards Dranesville?"

"How do you know that?" asked Sergeant Curtis, who marched beside his squad.

"We jess passed a coupla farms I remember seein' when we come here after the battle."

"But that don't make no gol-dang sense," fumed the sergeant. "Why would we be goin' west if we's ta be sent with Little Mac ta the Peninsula?"

"I never believed that rumor about us joining McClellan," said Jimmy. "After all, why would our generals let us in on their secret strategy? If we knew what they're planning, you can bet the Confederates would, too."

"What ya said makes too much sense fer our generals ta have thought o' it," laughed Boone. "I still think the sergeant's right 'bout the whole Peninsula idea. How 'bout you, Dan?"

Boone's comment sparked a debate that lasted for the next couple of miles of their march. They were passing through rich farm country, and only Comfort, Miles, and Starr made no guess as to their destination. Comfort was already too winded to waste his breath on conversation. Starr and Miles were busy studying every farmhouse, barn, and outbuilding that came into view.

"What's ya lookin' at, Starr?" growled Curtis after most of the men disagreed with the sergeant's Peninsula theory.

Starr stiffened but remained silent. Momentarily, he shifted his gaze to the back of the man marching in front of him.

"Like any weasel, he's lookin' fer a chicken coop full o' fat hens," said Frank.

Miles muttered something under his breath and then copied his friend's stance. When no one was able to ruffle the outcasts' feathers, the conversation shifted back to Union strategy.

The men continued to bicker until the weariness of their march silenced them. Bucky's haversack had long since become a burden, and Jimmy complained about his cramping legs. The sergeant developed blisters and limped painfully through the mud. Only Boone and Frank didn't seem any worse off for the walk. The lanky woodsmen pressed on mile after mile, craning their necks to see what would be around the next bend.

Curtis, Bucky, and Jimmy tramped wearily on until the ranks in front of them slowed and finally came to a complete stop.

"What's the holdup?" asked Jimmy to no one in particular.

"Look," answered the sergeant. "A supply wagon's stuck in the mud. I still can't figger what genius come up with the idea o' usin' gol-dang mules as draft animals."

"Yeah, Sergeant, them mules is the most contrary beasts on the face o' this green earth," chuckled Boone. "See that driver tryin' ta lead his team through a place they decided not ta go? He might jess as well try sweet-talkin' a schoolmarm outta her britches."

"Come on. Let's lend a hand," Bucky offered.

"Good idea," agreed Jimmy.

"Hold on there, boys," Boone cautioned. "Them teamsters can swear a blue streak. I heared one driver up in

Pennsylvany that cussed so bad that the August leaves turned their fall colors an' fell two months earlier than they shoulda."

"Cut the chatter, Boone. Close up," Sergeant Curtis ordered.

The men moved forward until they drew even with the bogged-down wagon where the teamster was pelting the air with curses from a foul, seemingly endless vocabulary. When he finally did get stuck for a new expletive, he merely rearranged the ones he previously used in a new, creative pattern. His oaths were accompanied by the practiced crack of the whip at the ears and heels of the lead animals. Although the little beasts danced and lunged, the wagon only sunk further into the muck.

"Don't that fella know he's wastin' his time 'til he gets them bigger animals next ta the wagon ta pull their weight?" observed Frank disgustedly.

"If you're such an expert," ordered the sergeant, "go over an' lend 'im a hand. The rest of you men, bend yer backs an' git that gol-dang wagon outta here. This sure ain't where we want ta make camp tonight, an' my blistered feet ain't gonna last through no night march ta git us to a better spot."

"Okay, Sergeant," Boone said. "But I'm warnin' you men. Don't git near the business end o' them mules. They kin kick in most any direction at any time, an' they'll put a hurtin' on ya sure as shootin'."

"Boone, I 'spose ya got a story 'bout that, too," mocked Frank.

"I do, Frank," said Boone, pushing for all he was worth, "but I can't grunt an' talk at the same time."

As ordered, the rest of the company positioned themselves around Boone to gain the leverage needed to move the wagon from its predicament. Once it was free, the brutes moved smartly down the trail with the teamster lashing them with both his tongue and black snake whip.

"Nice fella," Boone observed. "Didn't even say 'thanks'."

"Must be livin' with them stubborn mules makes a man forgit his manners," said Frank. "'Course, I'm livin' with some o' the army's orneriest brutes, an' I got the manners of a Philadelphia gent."

"The line forms here, Bucktails. Git movin'," barked Sergeant Curtis, pretending not to enjoy Frank's comment.

Finally, as evening approached, the officers decided to make camp near a tumble-down gristmill. Before the men were dismissed from the ranks, they were given new oilcloth raincoats from another supply wagon that had bogged down in a mud hole and had to be lightened of its cargo before it would budge.

After Bucky was handed his new coat, he grumbled to Jimmy, "Jess what I need. Somethin' else ta stick in my dang haversack."

"Be quiet, Bucky," joked his friend. "Now, you're starting to sound like Sergeant Curtis."

"Yeah, I wouldn't complain too loud about them raincoats," warned the issuing officer. "If you join three of 'em together, they'll make a dandy tent. That may be the only shelter you fellas have 'til next winter."

Bucky and his friends camped near a railroad embankment, which provided some shelter from the rising wind. There they found part of a discarded railroad tie, and they hacked it into pieces to feed a hungry fire. Starr and Miles sat by themselves over a smoky fire they made of green branches.

To make up for his recent standoffishness, Bucky volunteered to cook supper for his squad. He boiled a pot of coffee and roasted salt pork on a spit. He thought about making Skillygalee, but the men were too hungry to wait for hardtack to be soaked in cold water and fried brown in pork fat.

After they had wolfed down the sizzling meat, Comfort said, "Looks like it might get kinda cold tonight, Sergeant.

Ain't ya sorry that we didn't bring our good old Sibley tent with us on this here march?"

"What, an' be cooped up with you stinkin' fellas another night?" replied Curtis, nursing his blistered feet. "I'd rather be sleepin' in the fresh air by the open fire that you're gonna stay awake an' tend fer me."

"But, I'm a . . . corporal. Why don't ya order one of these privates ta do it fer ya?"

"Keep it up, an' I won't have ta look any further than you ta find me a private."

After the sergeant's outburst, the soldiers' sporadic conversations were interrupted by yawns and incomplete sentences. Finally, Bucky and the others spread their raincoats on the ground, wrapped themselves in their blankets, and fell into a dead sleep that charging cavalry wouldn't have disturbed.

The next morning Sergeant Curtis woke to find a shivering Comfort crouched over a pile of smoking embers. Crawling stiffly from his blanket, Curtis growled, "I thought I told ya ta keep that fire burnin'. Fell asleep, didn't ya?"

"No, sir, Sergeant. I didn't neglect my duty. I run outta wood."

"Well, we'll jess have ta git us some more. Culp. Crossmire. Crandall. Lemon. Get your be-hinds movin'. We got wood ta gather. Come along, Comfort. Unless, you're too tired from stayin' up all night, poor baby."

The sergeant led his foraging party through clumps of awakening soldiers, who stirred about like bees in a cold hive. Some men boiled coffee over smoldering fires. Others roamed about looking for something to burn. A few squads were using their raincoats to fashion crude tents. Another group of men was still trying to extricate the bogged-down supply wagon from the quagmire that had eaten it. Everywhere officers barked orders while they rode to and fro on their horses.

Bucky and the others pressed forward until they reached the abandoned gristmill on the outskirts of camp. Its roof had collapsed, and the stones of one wall littered the road. As they picked their way around this obstacle, a sentry stepped from the shadows and said, "Sergeant, where are ya takin' these men?"

"We're gonna do a little foragin' fer firewood. We used up what we had last night, an' the rest o' the camp is picked cleaner than a carcass gnawed by a flock o' turkey buzzards."

"Is that so? Are ya sure ya wasn't plannin' to raid a few hen houses while you was at it? Sorry, but Colonel McNeil has given orders that no one's allowed out of camp without a pass. The farmers hereabouts are friendly to the Union, an' the colonel wants to make sure they stay that way. He outlawed foragin' altogether."

"Well, what are we supposed ta do 'bout breakfast if we can't heat up coffee an' such?"

"You was issued three days of cooked rations. You'll jess have to eat 'em cold. An' there's always hardtack."

Grumbling, the sergeant led his squad back to their campsite, and they collapsed wearily near their haversacks. After awhile, Comfort gathered up his musket and other gear and stomped away, chomping on a hard biscuit that he didn't bother to check for weevils. He headed toward where Starr and Miles huddled over a tiny fire.

"Where are ya goin', Comfort?" asked Sergeant Curtis.

"He's jess livin' up ta his name," said Frank. "He'd rather be comfortable sittin' next ta a fire with them skunks than be with us cold, starvin' fellas."

The corporal ignored Frank's insult and joined Starr and Miles. Between bites of his biscuit, Comfort's lips mouthed angry words that elicited an equally angry response from his companions. Miles fixed Curtis with a murderous look and began frying some bacon. The delicious odor drifted across the camp while Starr gave an animated welcome to his new ally.

Rising menacingly to his feet, Curtis gnashed his teeth and growled like a cornered bruin. He continued to snarl even when Scarecrow, whistling cheerfully, came up the road lugging his drum. "H-H-Hi fellas," the boy said. "I . . . I . . . I been l-l-lookin' all over for ya. I . . . I . . . I got some g-g-good news."

"What's that?" grunted the sergeant.

"I . . . I . . . I got dis-m-m-missed from the d-d-drummers squad 'cause we's gonna be stayin' here for a few d-d-days. Colonel McNeil s-s-said so hisself."

"What's good about that?" asked Dan Lemon.

"T-T-That m-m-means we can r-r-rest."

"Rest," groaned Frank. "That's what we did the whole winter."

"Gol-dang McNeil. Why don't he git on with it? Or at least let us git some wood. Now, what's Starr doin'?"

Starr and his comrades finished breakfast and began erecting a tent against the railroad embankment that formed the northern boundary of the camp. They used their new oilcloth raincoats for the sides. Two muskets driven bayonet-first into the ground served as poles. After the tent was in place, they withdrew inside and began making all kinds of commotion.

"What are they doin' in there?" wondered the sergeant. "Diggin' a latrine? Come on, boys, let's go an' see if we kin scrounge up some firewood somewhere in this here camp. Maybe if they ain't pulled that supply wagon out o' the mud yet, we kin bust that up an' burn it."

Bucky, Scarecrow, and Jimmy combed the southern part of the camp while Curtis, Boone, Frank, and Lemon looked in the eastern section. Although they searched hard, they returned with only one small armful of wood apiece. What they gathered would be barely enough for one more night.

Starr, Miles, and Comfort, on the other hand, sat in front of a raging bonfire that shot flames high into the air. Each man sat roasting a whole chicken on a spit, and they were swilling cups of fresh milk. The smell of their feast attracted more than Sergeant Curtis' squad. A tall, bearded officer and his aide trotted up on their horses and dismounted to investigate.

"What's going on here?" inquired the bearded colonel. "Where did you men get that fresh food?"

"A farmer sold it ta us, Colonel McNeil, sir," said Starr with a grin. "It's a pleasure ta finally meet ya, sir. We got more chickens in our tent if you'd like one, sir."

"No farmers were allowed in camp. Where did you really get the food?"

"I know," said the aide, peering into the tent. "Come and look at this, Colonel McNeil."

The colonel walked over to the tent and found a tunnel through the railroad embankment where the back wall should have been. The tunnel came out beyond the camp where no sentries were posted. It was just wide enough for a heavy man like Comfort to worm through and provided easy access to the surrounding Virginia farms.

Outraged, Colonel McNeil turned and growled, "So you men deliberately disobeyed my order against foraging? What are your names?"

"Private Starr, sir."

"Private Miles, sir."

"Corporal Comfort, sir."

"*Private* Comfort, you and the others are to take down that tent and block up the tunnel. Then you are to report to headquarters for punishment. Each of you will be tied to a spare wagon wheel and put on display for the rest of the regiment. You will wear a sign saying 'Thief', so that all will know your offense."

"B-B-But, sir," sputtered Starr in disbelief. "How kin ya do this ta me after all the votes I rounded up fer ya in the e-lection? Why, I practically won ya the colonelcy."

"I don't care if you cast the deciding vote, soldier. No one disobeys my orders and goes unpunished."

Colonel McNeil signaled to Curtis and his squad. When they arrived at Starr's campsite, the colonel said, "Sergeant, I would like you to watch these three scoundrels while they fill in their tunnel. Afterward, bring them to my quarters under armed guard."

"Yes, sir."

"And, Sergeant. Make sure none of that food or firewood goes to waste."

"We sure will, Colonel McNeil."

Tied on a wheel;
Put on dis-play.
That is the end
O' my drinkin' today!

Bucktail reenactor Ben Miller is pictured in full combat gear, which weighs between forty and fifty pounds. Sadly, troops would shed their gear on long marches and suffer the consequences of want.

Chapter Eight

The Mud March

"Gol-dang weak-kneed generals," grumbled Sergeant Curtis on the fifth morning of their encampment near the gristmill. "Why can't they make up their flask-addled minds an' send us where we kin git outta this mud an' have a crack at them Rebs?"

The sergeant's words had barely died away before a bugle sounded assembly, and the Bucktails scrambled to pack their gear and get into marching formation. Again Scarecrow ran to join the other drummers to begin the roll beat that sent the division forward. The blisters and sore muscles were long healed, and the men stepped smartly back the way they had come, east toward Pierpont.

After five fatiguing miles, the division veered to the right and reached Difficult Creek, which was spanned by a spindly, log bridge. When the first Bucktails tramped onto the bridge, marching in step, it began to quake dangerously. Noting the effect of the pounding feet, Sergeant Curtis stopped his men from crossing just before the bridge collapsed in creaking slow motion. Many marchers were dumped into the swollen creek. The current was swift and deep from the spring runoff, and panicky swimmers ditched their muskets in their attempt to reach safety. They swam and thrashed back to the bank, reaching madly for the extended hands of their comrades. When the last of the swimmers was snatched from the icy water, a cheer rose from the ranks and prayers of thanks were mouthed by many lips.

While fires were being built to dry out the soaked, freezing soldiers, Bucky said, "Thanks, Sergeant. Ya really saved our bacon this time. I sure weren't ready for no bath on such a chilly mornin'."

"Maybe not," joked Boone, "but it woulda made ya smell a lot better."

"What are we gonna do now, Sergeant?" asked Jimmy. "I heard this shortcut would have saved a lot of marching."

"It looks like we'll have ta backtrack all the way ta gol-dang Pierpont. I'm jess glad no loaded wagons tried ta go across that rickety excuse fer a bridge. We'd be here five more days tryin' ta free 'em from the creek."

"Hey, I wish they had sent 'em across. Then maybe we'd be gettin' some new boots to go along with them raincoats," chuckled Boone. "Lord only knows Starr could use 'em. Look. He still ain't stitched up the ones he's got on."

After the dunked soldiers had dried themselves by the fire, sure enough the division retraced its steps to the main road and headed toward their winter camp. A steady drizzle turned into a downpour, dousing the men's spirits as well. The unyielding mud made the march a test of patience and endurance. Soon all conversation, even the cursing, stopped cold. The Bucktails, however, plodded on until they reached a fork in the road. Here, the officers huddled for a few minutes before leading the column to the right, away from the shelter of Camp Pierpont. Their decision precipitated a new outburst of cursing that continued until Captains Blanchard, McDonald, and Taylor subdued it with barked orders and the flats of their swords.

The division marched until dark, covering twenty-five miles in the mud and rain. Most of the men were ready to collapse by the time orders were given to fall out and find shelter. Their uniforms were completely soaked through and weighed heavily on their bowed shoulders. Sergeant Curtis' blisters were back. Jimmy's legs were racked with cramps. Even Boone and Frank, the sturdy woodsmen, limped noticeably.

The division had reached Falls Church, and luckily Bucky was not too exhausted to scout for a campsite out of the mud. After leaving his soaked haversack with Jimmy, he sloshed on through the town, climbed a little rise, and discovered a camp recently abandoned by Union soldiers bound for the Peninsula. The camp was complete with pitched tents. Some had stoves still in place. He rubbed his eyes to make sure he was seeing right before he sloshed back to tell his friends. The word passed quickly among Curtis' squad, and soon they were filing off through the darkness behind Bucky. That is, everybody except Starr, Miles, and Comfort who were still under the watchful eye of Colonel McNeil.

"Gol-dang it, Bucky," shouted Curtis when he spotted the tents in the gloom. "I oughta make ya corporal fer findin' these here canvas hotels."

"I thought ya was glad ta be sleepin' out in the open again, Sergeant," said Dan Lemon. "Are ya sure ya wanna share a tent with us stinkin' fellas?"

"If it weren't rainin' so hard, I wouldn't. This time I'll jess have ta rough it."

Frank, Bucky, and Jimmy laughed as they rushed to the first Sibley tent with a stove. There was even firewood inside and some dry blankets. Frank had a fire roaring up the stovepipe in no time, and the shivering men huddled with their backs pressed against the firebox. Steam rose from their sodden jackets, and the smell of wet wool was pungent in their nostrils. Thoughts of supper came much later, after the numbness left their hands and feet.

The next morning found the tent littered with drying clothes and men wrapped in warm blankets. The bugles that blew assembly did not awaken the snoring squad of Bucktails, nor did the drums that signaled the division's departure. Bucky was the first to open his eyes, and he rose to cook breakfast for his still-sleeping comrades. Only when the tantalizing aroma of brewing coffee filled the tent did the others crawl stiffly from their bedrolls.

"By golly, Bucky, you're gonna make someone a fine wife someday," joshed Boone. "What else are we gonna have besides that rotgut you call coffee?"

"Well, I shoved a few taters in the oven along with some bread that stayed dry in the bottom o' my haversack."

"Hey, even you can't ruin bread er taters," said Frank, "so it looks like this should be a dandy meal."

"I wish Sam could be here to enjoy this breakfast," added Jimmy. "I hope he's doing okay bivouacked with the other drummers."

"An' I'm jess glad Bucky didn't cook us no sassages," snickered Boone. "Green, seasoned sassages bought from some Dutch farmer."

After breakfast, the Bucktails took their time putting on their dry clothes and boots. They lingered to swap jokes and tease Bucky about his culinary skills. They also spent time tending their muskets, which had received a thorough soaking during the march. Each soldier carefully oiled and recharged his weapon before the squad headed back to where the rest of the division had bedded down in the muck.

"Where did everyone go?" gasped Jimmy when they found the division campsite vacant.

"I thought that was a giant burp I heared awhile back," replied Boone with a wink. "It looks like the mud swallowed the whole dang division."

"Not if these tracks are any indication," said Frank. "They's headin' straight down the road ta Alexandria. They musta pulled out while we was enjoyin' them fine accommodations over yonder."

The Bucktails shouldered their muskets and hurried along after the Union army for an hour before they caught up with the rear guard. When challenged by the patrol, Boone shouted, "Sorry we're late, but our sergeant here caught us a buncha water moccasins fer breakfast, an' we couldn't break camp 'til we had ourselves a regular feast. We musta undercooked 'em though, 'cause we could feel 'em squirmin' all the way down. The sergeant still has a couple of them snakes left if you boys would be interested. Go ahead. Reach right there in his haversack."

The guards just shook their heads and motioned for the stragglers to pass. Sergeant Curtis' men filtered through the ranks until they reached their usual spot in line and fell in cadence with the others. Ahead through the trees, they could see the city of Alexandria sprawled along the banks of the broad Potomac River. The white sails of troop transports were plainly visible, and the backwoodsmen gawked at them with amazement and delight.

"I hope we's on one of them gol-dang ships by tomorrow," said Curtis. "The sooner we's headin' for the Peninsula, the better I'll like it."

"Me, too," said Frank. "It's sure gonna beat stompin' through all this mud."

"I ain't too sure 'bout sailin'," grunted Dan Lemon. "What if I get seasick?"

"How can ya git sick of somethin' you ain't even seen yet?" cracked Boone.

The Bucktails marched to a camp outside of Alexandria. There they stood at attention on the parade ground to be reviewed by Colonel McNeil and Lieutenant Colonel Kane. The two officers looked disturbed to Bucky as they trotted back and forth on their mud-spattered horses.

Finally, the colonel, with a long tug on his beard, said, "Men, I just received word that we have been assigned to the First Corps commanded by General McDowell. It will be our responsibility to form a buffer between the Confederates and Washington. We will not be shipped to Fortress Monroe as originally planned. President Lincoln himself requested that our prestigious regiment be kept behind to guard the capital from possible attack, while General McClellan presses up the Peninsula toward Richmond. Make yourselves comfortable, men. We are to wait here in Alexandria for further orders. Dismissed."

Stunned, Bucky and his friends stumbled muttering out of line, faced with the grim prospect of trying to get comfortable in a windswept, flat field of a camp without proper tents or provisions. It started to pour again, too, and Bucky huddled with Jimmy and Sergeant Curtis in an attempt to combine their oilcloth raincoats into some kind of serviceable shelter. The tent they assembled on a frail sapling frame was barely big enough for the three of them to squeeze into. When the sergeant stretched out full length, his feet and legs stuck well out into the rain.

"What kind o' gol-dang doghouse is this?" grumbled Curtis.

"After this storm passes, we can fix it a little better," said Jimmy. "You can get us passes into Alexandria, and we'll buy some canvas to lengthen it out."

"Buy canvas? With what? We ain't seen one red cent from the paymaster since January. If my lumber boss had taken this long ta pay me, I'd have quit him long be-fore now."

"Maybe tomorrow we'll get our pay and orders to move somewhere better," replied Jimmy. "I'll pray about it before I go to sleep."

"Pray all ya want. It ain't gonna happen."

"Colonel McNeil didn't seem no happier than us 'bout gettin' stuck in Alexandria," said Bucky. "What do you fellas think o' him as our leader?"

"I sure liked the way he whacked Starr an' them other weasels," grinned Curtis. "I 'specially enjoyed watchin' Comfort fill in their tunnel under the railroad. I weren't sure what made 'im sweat more—workin' a shovel er worryin' 'bout his punishment."

"That convinced me we'll get a fair shake from the colonel," said Jimmy. "I now respect Hugh McNeil almost as much as I do Thomas Kane."

"That goes fer me, too," agreed Bucky.

Chapter Nine

CAN'T MAKE A CROOKED STICK STRAIGHT

Bucky and his friends still found themselves in Alexandria at the end of March. The weather grew warmer each day until he, Jimmy, and Scarecrow were able to send their overcoats home to the Jewetts in Smethport. The grass came up, and the camp was full of songbirds that daily woke Bucky well before reveille. Then he would crawl out of his doghouse tent to watch the sun rise over the glittering Potomac River and dream of his woodland home. Bucky hated this part of Virginia, and being confined to the Union camp made him feel like a prisoner. What he truly longed for were endless mountain ridges and glens full of fat deer. What he truly needed were groves of hemlocks where a hunter could revel in his solitude.

One morning when Bucky was sitting outside, he saw Starr, Miles, and another scrawny rascal come slinking back to Company I carrying their haversacks and muskets. They erected their doghouse off by itself and huddled together in a grumbling clump around a smoky fire. The third man was Comfort, who had lost an incredible amount of weight. Bucky didn't recognize him until his voice rose angrily to denounce his recent punishment meted out by Colonel McNeil. "How could he work us like he done after tyin' us on wheels an' brandin' us thieves in front o' the whole regiment?" howled the private. "An' he took my stripes, too, dang his hide. An' ordered me 'round like a convict. If I'm ever alone with that stinkin' colonel, I'll make him pay. Why, I'll take him an'—"

The wind blew away the rest of Comfort's words, and Bucky started his own breakfast fire. Soon the surrounding tents emptied, and Boone, Frank, Jimmy, Scarecrow, Sergeant Curtis, and Dan Lemon turned to stare at the returning soldiers of their squad.

"Well, I'll be danged," said Frank. "Starr an' them other skunks has been gone so long, I figgered they either deserted er got court-martialed."

"From what I overheard Comfort say," added Bucky, "it seems they was part o' some work gang."

"That skinny fella's Comfort?" asked Dan. "They musta starved him some ta get him that thin."

"They might be done with their punishments," warned the sergeant, "but we best still keep an eye on them fellas. In the meantime, let's eat."

"All we got is grits an' beans," grumbled Dan, "along with salt pork so strong it'd curl Colonel Kane's beard."

"What I wouldn't give fer a nice hunk o' venison ta gnaw on," said Frank, "an' a mess o' boiled leeks. Let them flatlanders keep their stinkin' pork."

After breakfast a bugle blared assembly, and the men shouldered their muskets and stamped to the parade ground. They hurried into rank, and Captain Blanchard ordered the company to attention. When the rest of the regiment had followed suit, there was a roll of drums, and an officer limped onto the field to the whistles and cheers of Company E. Bucky recognized the wan man as Captain Niles, who had been wounded at Dranesville. He gave Company E a smart salute and assumed command from the first lieutenant. The lieutenant returned the salute and then, in his excitement, shook Niles' hand like a pump handle.

The drums struck a marching cadence, and Colonel McNeil rode to the head of the regiment and began barking orders. He flawlessly led the Bucktails through a series of intricate drills that transformed the marching column into a battle line. He ended the exercise by ordering the companies back into formation for some close order drills. Back and forth the regiment marched—to the front, to the rear, to the right, to the left. Next, the colonel went through the manual of arms and personally inspected each man's musket. All went off without a flaw, and, to Bucky, Colonel McNeil looked exceedingly pleased.

Bucky also noticed that Lieutenant Colonel Kane observed the exercises from a distance. The lieutenant colonel studied the battle maneuvers carefully, but the rote close order drills did not hold his attention for long. Instead, the officer's gaze shifted to the north, and he fidgeted in his saddle, tracing the scar beneath his beard with a gloved hand.

Boy, Bucky thought, I'll bet Colonel Kane is dreamin' o' home jess like us privates. He must miss his wife an' children somethin' awful. Or maybe he's thinkin' 'bout Dranesville er some other battle. He ain't much of a parade ground officer, but he sure is a fightin' wildcat.

The monotony of camp life was intensified now by daily drills conducted by Colonel McNeil. The regiment was in the middle of a wheeling maneuver one April afternoon when a messenger galloped his spent mount onto the field and conferred briefly with the colonel. McNeil immediately canceled the maneuver and said, "Men, we've been ordered to march to the Orange and Alexandria Railroad. Break camp and report back here in one hour. Dismissed."

It only took Bucky and the others of his squad a half hour to tear down their doghouses, pack their haversacks, and scramble back into formation. While they waited for the other companies to return, Bucky asked, "Does this mean we's been called ta the Peninsula?"

"I don't think so," replied Sergeant Curtis. "The gol-dang railroad we's gonna ride goes ta Manassas Junction."

"If that train's anything like the one we took ta Harrisburg when we en-listed, I'd rather walk ta Manassas," grumbled Frank.

"What do you fellas think?" asked Boone, nodding to Starr, Miles, and Comfort, who had just crept into line. "Would you rather ride ta Manassas er walk?"

When none of the trio offered an opinion, Frank said, "Maybe Comfort's tongue shrunk so small it don't work no more. I still can't git over how powerful skinny he got."

Comfort glared at Frank but did not break the silence. Miles and Starr wouldn't speak either, so the rest of the squad began cursing cramped boxcars and train rides in general. Their fit of swearing continued the length of the march and grew to a crescendo at the railroad depot.

When the engine clanked and chugged into view, Sergeant Curtis growled, "Look at that gol-dang steam maker. The way it's hissin', it reminds me o' a teapot on wheels."

"An' look at them boxcars," groused Lemon. "We'll be packed in like cattle headin' fer a slaughterhouse by the time all o' us gits aboard."

Before the train came to a full stop, Starr and his cronies leaped into the first boxcar and squatted in a corner by themselves. They glared out through the slats at Sergeant Curtis and Frank before holding a malicious powwow.

Bucky and Jimmy had to practically drag Scarecrow up to the train. He kept staring with trepidation at the smoke-spewing engine and jumped back with a frightened bleat when the engineer blew the whistle.

"Come on, Sam," pleaded Jimmy. "If we don't hurry, we'll get stuck sitting in the middle of the car with soldiers that will fall on us every time the train stops."

"Yeah, ya don't wanna git squished flat before we git ta Manassas, do ya?" asked Bucky.

"I . . . I . . . I ain't never been t-t-this close to no t-t-train before," stammered Sam, "I-I-let alone r-r-rode one."

Scarecrow continued to hang back until Sergeant Curtis growled, "Private Whalen, git yer be-hind up them steps before I boot it up. If ya don't wanna ride with yer squad, maybe I kin arrange a seat fer ya up on the roof."

Scarecrow's eyes got very wide, and he scrambled into the boxcar like he'd been bayoneted in the rear. Jimmy, Bucky, and Sergeant Curtis followed closely on his heels. By the time the four of them entered, however, there was only one space left beside Boone and Frank and a larger area near Starr and his henchmen. The sergeant plopped heavily down next to Boone, so Bucky and the other two boys were forced to pick their way over to Starr's corner.

They barely got situated when the train lurched into motion. Immediately, Sam began quivering and making strangling noises in his throat. As the blood drained from Sam's face, he grabbed hold of Jimmy's arm and squeezed until Jimmy cried out in pain.

"Ya know, fellas," said Starr sarcastically to his cronies, "I ain't seen nobody act like them two since the last re-vival meetin' I attended. I only went ta impress a gal an' ta laugh at them dang holy rollers."

"What's wrong, Scarecrow?" asked Miles. "This big, bad train got ya spooked? Poor baby."

"Don't wet yer britches, Scarecrow," hissed Comfort, "or we'll be pitchin' ya out the door like a wet bale o' hay."

"Yeah, you're nothin' but a sissy," added Starr. "An' I don't like sittin' with sissies. Keep up that whinin', an' like my partner said, you'll be marchin' ta Manassas yet."

Sam grew so scared that his breath came in short spasms, and he looked ready to vomit. Bucky whispered words of encouragement while Jimmy snapped at Starr, "Why don't you leave my friend alone? You're only making things worse."

"Ya can't tell me an' my partners what ta do. We don't listen ta sissies."

"An' what are ya gonna do 'bout it if we don't lay off Scarecrow?" snarled Miles. "Bore us ta death readin' from yer Bible?"

"No, but I'm liable to put my foot on your throat. I put up with bullies like you before I became a Bucktail, but no more. I proved my mettle at Dranesville while you were lost in the woods, Starr. If you fellows don't shut your mouths, I'm going to save the Rebels the trouble of blowing holes in you."

Starr flushed crimson, and a sarcastic reply died on his lips. Miles and Comfort grumbled but shut their mouths. Bucky, meanwhile, smiled proudly at Jimmy while Scarecrow stared at him in awe.

The rest of the trip passed uneventfully, with Starr and his cronies staring out the boxcar slats at the passing Virginia farmland. Scarecrow settled down enough to doze while Jimmy and Bucky whispered about the adventures they had had since leaving Smethport.

"Can you believe it's been a whole year since we left home?" wondered Jimmy aloud.

"Yeah, it's mighty hard ta figger all right. We both come a long way since then, but 'specially you, Jimmy," replied Bucky with a grin. "You've growed into a real fine man."

It was dark when the train wheezed into Manassas, and the engineer switched onto a siding to wait for dawn. The Bucktails slept where they sat until the sun sliced through the boxcar slats to wake them the next morning. Orders rang from outside, and the soldiers rose stiffly and were greeted by a bitter cold when they exited the train. During the night a foot of snow had fallen, and the Bucktails cursed and grumbled when ordered to pitch camp among the drifts.

Bucky noticed that Starr, Miles, and Comfort seemed awfully interested in another army train that was parked at a different siding. The three rascals eyed the baggage cars and whispered among themselves while erecting their doghouse.

When the rest of the unit filed off to roll call, Starr and his cronies slipped aboard the army train, and Bucky followed at a safe distance to see what mischief they were up to. He could hear them rooting around inside while he crept up the steps of the first baggage car. Peering in the door, Bucky could barely make out the three soldiers in the half-light of the windowless interior. They were examining a box, and Starr struck a match to read the label.

"Well, I'll be danged," whispered Starr excitedly. "I was right. It is addressed ta the Medical Di-rector. Careful now, boys. We don't wanna damage what's inside."

Miles drew his knife, and Bucky could hear the blade grating against the wooden top. The top slid off after much effort, and Comfort withdrew a bottle that he held in Starr's match light so he could read its label.

"Why, Starr, it is whiskey. There's a dozen bottles here. An' the label says, 'Fer hospital use.' I got a sore, thirsty throat that this here whiskey'll cure jess fine."

"Hey, look," whispered Miles, stifling a laugh. "There's another box jess like it. Strike a match, Jeb, an' we'll see if it's whiskey, too."

"Don't need ta bother with that. Take my word fer it, boys. It's the same as what we got here."

The men broke open the second box, and Miles and Comfort withdrew dark bottles and held them jubilantly in the air.

"Come on, join us, Jeb," said Comfort. "Let's have ourselves a little toast ta celebrate our find."

"Bottoms up," added Miles, not waiting to clink bottles with the others.

Comfort, also, began drinking right away. He chugged the contents to the bottom before Starr could even take a swig. Starr hoisted his bottle, but it was slapped away by

Miles, who stood clutching his throat in a grotesque fashion. "It's not bitters, not bitters," he choked.

Comfort began gasping for air and clawing at the side of the car. He reeled drunkenly before he collapsed in a heap. Miles keeled over, too, and Starr spit out the liquid in his mouth and uttered, "What the hell?"

Bucky climbed into the baggage car during the confusion and grabbed Starr roughly by the arm. Starr lashed out with his right fist that caught Bucky square in the ear. Bucky gasped in surprise, and Starr squirmed out of his grasp. Before he could grab him a second time, the rascal pushed Bucky over backward, leaped from the car, and plowed off through the snow.

Bucky struggled to his feet and rushed to find his squad. They were lined up in formation practicing the manual of arms when he sprinted up to Captain Blanchard and stammered, "C-C-Come quick, sir. Bring the men. S-S-Starr's run off. Comfort an' Miles might be . . . dead."

Blanchard wasted no time dismissing the company, and they scurried after Bucky to the army train. "Comfort . . . Miles . . . inside," puffed Bucky, pointing to the car they had pillaged. "Starr ran that way. Hurry! Before he gets away."

Captain Blanchard signaled for Sergeant Curtis' squad to chase Starr and then followed Bucky onto the train. The captain found a lantern hanging near the baggage car entrance and struck a match to light it. Even though Bucky knew what to expect, he still jumped when the lantern light revealed Miles' and Comfort's grotesquely twisted faces. They were dead all right. No one had to feel for a pulse to see that.

"I'll be danged," said Captain Blanchard as he examined the bodies. "What happened to these men, Culp?"

"They drunk somethin' outta dark bottles they stoled from that box near Miles' head. They thought it was whiskey."

The captain picked up one of the empty bottles that was lying where Comfort had collapsed. "The label says 'Laudanum.' That's got opium in it. No wonder the poor devils died so quick. After all the punishments they received, they should have known better than to pull something like this."

Blanchard and Bucky left the baggage car, and the officer assembled a burial party to tend to Comfort's and Miles' bodies. The captain also asked Bucky to accompany him to headquarters, so he could fill out his report. It took most of the morning for Bucky to answer questions the officers had for him there. He even had to tell his story to Colonel McNeil, who pulled on his beard and muttered, "I hate to say this, but I guess you can't make a crooked stick straight no matter how you try."

When darkness slipped over the countryside, the search party straggled dejectedly back into camp with no prisoner in tow. Although these men were veteran woodsmen, adept at tracking even the wiliest of creatures, Starr had somehow given them the slip. As Sergeant Curtis put it, "Starr is like a gol-dang ghost. We followed his tracks in the snow fer about an hour, an' then they disappeared. He headed north like we figgered he would. At least fer awhile. Later he started weavin' through the thickest brush ya kin imagine. After that, he stomped up a creek an' across some slippery rocks. Where we lost 'im, though, was when he got on railroad tracks goin' north 'n' south. We went north an' never did run back onto his trail. Where Starr went, I got no clue. Wherever it is, I hope the gol-dang rascal is cold, hungry, an' miserable."

Chapter Ten

MR. LINCOLN

The Bucktails' advance south from Manassas was tediously slow, and the regiment spent nearly a month plodding in the general direction of Fredericksburg. Sometimes Bucky and his squad covered twenty miles in a day while other days they only marched one mile. Some weeks they made great progress while other weeks they sulked in their doghouses for days on end. This irregular movement left the men scratching their heads, cursing their generals, and deploring their bad luck.

One bright April morning the Bucktails tramped along breathing in the fragrant aroma of the dogwood blossoms. They marched in silence admiring the beauty of the day until Sergeant Curtis said, "Ya know, fellas, I jess can't git that gol-dang Starr outta my mind. The way he vanished, I think the devil hisself took that rascal."

"He must be mighty agile ta have walked them train rails like he done," added Boone. "I never seen nothin' like it. How could anyone go four miles without slippin' even once an' leavin' a footprint er two behind?"

"Yeah," agreed Frank. "I done a lot o' trackin' in my time, an' I ain't never had a critter give me the slip like that. I figgered we'd catch Starr fer sure when I saw the de-stinct tracks his split boots made in the snow."

"He couldn't have been much of a cobbler," scoffed Jimmy, "if he couldn't even stitch up his own soles."

"Yeah, but ya gotta remember, Jimmy, Starr didn't take much care o' his other soul neither," chuckled Boone.

"Why did ya let 'im get away anyhow, Bucky?" grumbled Curtis. "Colonel McNeil woulda hung him after all the other mischief he done."

"Like ya said, Sergeant. Starr's a mighty slippery fella. It was plenty dark in that baggage car, an' once he squirmed outta my grip, I couldn't see no other part of 'im ta latch on to."

"Did any of you try tracking him south once you lost his trail on the railroad grade?"

"Jimmy, why would he wanna go into Reb territory?" asked Frank. "That don't make no sense fer a coward like Starr."

"Hey, didn't we jess pass a sign sayin' 'Falmouth' awhile back?" asked the sergeant. "There it is. Right ahead through the trees."

The Bucktails entered the sleepy southern village of Falmouth and drew up in the town square. While the soldiers formed into ranks, Colonel McNeil slumped over the neck of his horse. His face was flushed beneath his black beard, and Bucky heard the colonel's orderly say, "Sir, you're burning up. We better get you to a doctor. Looks like the fever to me."

Lieutenant Colonel Kane rode over to McNeil and offered the same diagnosis. After the orderly led the colonel away, Kane inspected the regiment and ordered it to set up camp in an open field next to the Rappahannock River.

Bucky, Jimmy, and Sam erected a doghouse at the river's edge next to Frank, Boone, and Curtis' tent. There they shared a fire and swapped outrageous yarns.

"Ain't this a nice place ta camp?" asked Boone. "It kinda reminds me o' fishin' the Allegheny River. Up there the pike an' bass is so plentiful a fella don't even need a pole. He kin catch 'em with his bare hands."

"I wouldn't wanna stick my bare hands in no pike's gills," said Curtis. "They's razor sharp."

"Who said anything 'bout usin' their gills?"

"W-W-Well, you ain't g-g-gonna g-g-grab 'em by the jaw. Their t-t-teeth is like d-d-daggers," stammered Sam.

"Yeah," added Bucky. "Don't ya mean ya netted them pike er gaffed 'em? That's how the Iroquois fish."

"Heck, all Boone would have ta do is take a bath in the river," laughed Frank, "an' the fish would float belly up. Then he'd have no trouble haulin' 'em out with his bare hands."

"Ha. Ha," replied Boone sarcastically. "Now, I'll bet ya won't believe I caught a six-foot muskie neither. That time I did use a pole. That rascal fought fer two hours before I drug him up on the bank. When I opened him up, I found he'd jess swallowed a full-growed snappin' turtle. What a feast I had! Not only did I gorge on de-licious muskie filets, but I also made me a big pot o' turtle soup."

"Boone, that ain't no fishin' story at all," lectured Curtis. "Why, I knew a fella who wanted ta git out o' the army real bad so he could be with his wife who was big with their first child. So he takes his rifle, fixes his bayonet, puts fishin' tackle on it, an' goes fishin' jess as big as ya please."

"What's so odd about that?" asked Jimmy. "I've seen lots of soldiers down by the river doing the same thing. They even caught some nice bass."

"I seen 'em, too, but this soldier was fishin' in mud puddles right in the middle o' camp," Curtis explained. "He'd jig a puddle fer a spell an' then move on to another puddle. The whole regiment was watchin' him before long, includin' the brass an' the army doctor. Finally, the doc tried ta git him ta stop the tomfoolery. Thing was, the fella would have none o' it."

"Probably catchin' too many fish," Boone scoffed.

"Even the captain an' the colonel asked the fella what he was fishin' fer, but they got no reply neither," Curtis continued, after fixing Boone with a warning glare. "The soldier kept right on fishin' like it was the most natural thing ta do." "Sergeant, ya sure ya ain't jess reelin' us in?" asked Bucky.

"No, I'm givin' it to ya straight. Jess like it happened. Well, anyhow, the fella kept on fishin' fer the next two days 'til the doc finally de-clares him unfit fer duty an' goes ta draw up the soldier's discharge papers."

"Dang, Curtis, this is the longest story I ever heared told," Boone taunted. "Can't ya git ta the point?"

"Okay . . . Okay! So an orderly de-livers them papers ta the fisherman, an' ya know what he says, Boone?"

"No, Sergeant. Tell us. P-l-l-ease."

"The fisherman says, 'Thank you. This is what I been fishin' fer all along.' Then the fella run ta his tent, got his personal belongin's, an' skipped outta camp the happiest man on the face o' this green earth."

"Well, I'll be," Boone groaned. "That story did have an end ta it. Jess too bad it weren't closer ta the beginnin'."

Despite Boone's and Curtis' tall tales, Bucky and his squad enjoyed their stay at Falmouth. The weather was pleasant and the food plentiful. Their pay finally came, and they supplemented their army rations with hams, potatoes, crackers, pies, and cheese that they bought from the local farmers. Besides, Boone actually fingered a few fish from the river and baked them for his friends on the campfire coals.

The McKean County boys enjoyed their new leadership, too. Colonel McNeil did have typhoid fever, and Lieutenant Colonel Kane took over temporary command of the regiment. They held no close order drills with Kane in charge but instead practiced the new system of tactics he devised at Camp Pierpont. The rest of the time, Bucky's squad basked in the sun, ate their fill, sang patriotic songs, and swapped gossip.

Near the end of May, Kane sent an order through his captains that the men were to shine their uniforms and weapons for a regimental review. While Sergeant Curtis' squad spit-polished their gear for the special inspection, Boone crowed, "I heared that President Lincoln is comin'." "An' jess how do ya know that?" challenged Frank. "Well, the other day I was havin' coffee with some fellas from Company G. Now, ya know that Captain McDonald's boys have a way o' knowin' jess 'bout everything that comes an' goes at headquarters."

"They sure do," Bucky snickered. "How many times have they had us movin' out ta fight the Rebs? 'Bout twice a week, I'd say."

"Yeah, and weren't they the ones who said our pay was coming while we were bivouacked at the gristmill?" needled Jimmy.

"Never mind them little lapses," Boone insisted. "I know Company G's right 'bout Mr. Lincoln's visit. Why, I'd bet my next pay on it."

"That's a safe bet," said Dan Lemon. "By the time it comes, we'll be too stinkin' old ta remember even bein' in Falmouth."

"I also learned somethin' else from McDonald's boys, but seein' how it's jess talk, I'll keep it ta myself," pouted Boone.

"Boone, if it's one thing I learned 'bout ya, it's that ya can't keep nothin' ta yerself," Sergeant Curtis offered. "Now, let's hear it. What are you an' Abe Lincoln plottin' these days?"

"No," Boone said. "You boys kin find out fer yerselves. But when the orders come down, don't say you're surprised."

"Boone, my patience is 'bout wore thin as the seat o' my britches," bellowed Curtis. "You tell us. That's an order."

"Hold yer fire, Sergeant. No need ta pull rank. I was buildin' fer suspense. Here's what I learned. First off, Mr. Lincoln's son, Willie, died in February. The president an' his wife was really struck low by this, 'specially Mrs. Lincoln."

"I read 'bout that," Lemon recalled. "It were some kinda fever from drinkin' bad water. The boy's death really tore up the president. Seems the other lad was sick, too."

"You mean Tad," Boone said, only too happy to embellish on the subject. "Well, Tad pulled through, an' that was a real blessin' 'cause he's quite the joker 'round the White House. It seems that one time Tad went ta see Mr. Stanton—"

"Who's that?" interrupted Frank, trying to deflate his know-it-all friend.

"Jess the secretary o' war is all. As I was sayin', young Tad asked ta be made an officer. Mr. Stanton, who ain't opposed ta a bit of fun, give the lad a commission. So what does Tad do? He up an' requisitions guns from the arsenal, dismisses the security guards at the White House, an' makes the White House staff the new guard. That's an officer who gits things done!"

"What in the devil does that have ta do with the president comin' here?" asked Frank disgustedly.

"Boone, this sure sounds like another one o' yer yarns," Dan groaned.

"This here story has lots ta do with the president comin'," Boone fired back. "Heck, the man's weighed down by personal tragedy, ta say nothin' o' this war, an' yet he still finds time ta visit the likes o' us."

"What else did you hear?"

"Somethin' you'd like ta know, Bucky. Seems that Mr. Lincoln is a gen-uine marksman. He loves his Spencer rifle an' puts a shot most anywhere he's aimin'. He has a range behind the White House an' loves ta practice."

"Gol-dang it, Boone, ya jess can't stay on track, can ya?" grumbled Curtis. "Ya still haven't told us *why* the president's comin'."

"From what McDonald's boys said, he's here ta review some real fightin' men. Dranesville's one o' the few victories chalked up by the North, an' we're the ones who won that there battle. He's also supposed ta be madder than a cornered wolverine at Little Mac. Rumor has it the president calls the Army o' the Potomac 'McClellan's Body Guard.'"

"So I guess he wants ta see fer hisself if the Union army has any spine ta it," Curtis said.

"That makes sense," agreed Bucky. "We've been sittin' on our backsides fer too long. Maybe Honest Abe will finally allow us ta do some fightin'."

"Boone, ya might jess as well told us that the president has a beard," said Frank sarcastically. "Yer big news is jess like yer fish stories."

"Okay, that's enough chatter," ordered Sergeant Curtis. "Let's git ta work an' make Mr. Lincoln remember the Bucktails."

The bugler blew assembly after lunch, and Bucky and Jimmy rushed to join Company I which gathered on the Falmouth road. When all the companies had fallen into rank, Lieutenant Colonel Kane marched them to the town square, where they turned smartly to face an imposing figure dressed in a black suit. The man had a bushy, black beard but no mustache, and his face was furrowed with a pensive expression. Wearing a stovepipe hat, he fairly towered over his personal guard. To Bucky, the man looked seven feet tall. Now this, he thought, is a man fit to be a president.

Kane called the men to attention and then accompanied President Lincoln as he strode from company to company to review the regiment. Upon completing his inspection, the president cleared his throat and said: "Men of Pennsylvania, I salute you. Your bravery at Dranesville is legendary, and your victory raised the spirits of many in need of buoying up. Wear your bucktails proudly, men, and help crush the Confederate menace that has torn our nation asunder."

After the president climbed aboard his carriage and, surrounded by cavalry, whisked away, Lieutenant Colonel

Kane also addressed the troops. "Men," he thundered, "our battle orders have finally arrived. Companies A, B, D, E, F, and K will proceed with Major Stone to join General McClellan's advance on Richmond. Companies C, G, H, and I will join me under General Bayard's command. We move out tomorrow. That's all. Dismissed."

Bucky, Jimmy, and the rest of the squad rushed jubilantly back to camp jabbering like magpies. The river sparkled with sunlight, and the afternoon warmth seemed to waken the men's lust for battle as much as the news they had received.

"Well, I'll be gol-danged," shouted Sergeant Curtis. "We's finally gonna see some action."

"Yeah," said Frank, "but why are they dividin' us Bucktails into two units? That makes me kinda nervous."

"Not me," said Boone. "I'm jess glad ta have Lieutenant Colonel Kane commandin' us. Now we won't have ta waste all that time salutin' an' drillin' in line like we done with McNeil. I'm hungry fer some real fightin', an' Kane has a nose fer it."

"I think we'll be a better unit without the rest of the regiment," assured Jimmy, "because now we'll only be with those most loyal to the lieutenant colonel."

"You're right," agreed Curtis. "The boys from Cameron, Elk, an' Chester Counties did give Kane the most votes fer colonel back at Pierpont. Like us McKean men, they'll follow him into a quicksand bog if he asks 'em."

"Boy," said Jimmy, his eyes widening with awe, "I still can't believe that Boone was right and that the president himself came all the way from Washington to see our regiment."

"See, Jimmy, I told ya he weren't the usual glad-handin' politician," said Boone. "I also heard Mr. Lincoln went ta Fredericksburg first ta see General McDowell an' that he took a whole mess o' high rankin' fellas with 'im. Ya didn't see none o' them other muckamucks come along ta visit us, did ya?"

"They was probably too busy drinkin' McDowell's whiskey," grumbled Curtis. "Us fightin' men's the ones with the dry throats, but do ya think them generals would even give us one little sip? The only reason I signed the muster roll is 'cause Captain Blanchard promised us a rum ration. The only booze I smelled since was that comin' out of a hospital tent."

"I'll bet Mr. Lincoln isn't a drinking man," replied Jimmy, "and you can't deny that he's an impressive-looking gentleman."

"Yes siree," said Frank. "I don't believe I've ever seen someone quite that tall. It's a good thing he ain't a general. Towerin' over us men the way he does, he'd be an easy target fer some Reb sniper."

"I'm glad we have such a big fella fer our president," said Bucky. "The Iroquois always chose the strongest, wisest man fer chief, an' now I see that the whites must do likewise."

"Hey, not ta change the subject er nothin'," interrupted Frank, "but didn't Kane say we'd be joinin' up with General Bayard? Ain't he in charge o' cavalry?"

"Yeah," said Sergeant Curtis. "They's nicknamed 'the Flyin' Brigade' 'cause o' the way they cover ground."

"What's the sense o' that?"

"I guess the generals in Washington wanna see if Kane's tactics will work. If us riflemen kin keep up with them gol-dang Flyin' Brigade boys, we'll do the lieutenant colonel proud."

"We best have ourselves a big supper," said Boone, "'cause we might not get much o' a chance ta eat with all the marchin' ahead o' us."

"Then you better get back down to the river and start fishing," said Jimmy.

"An' this time, Boone, remember ta use a pole," chuckled Frank.

"Why should he start now?" asked Bucky.

"'Cause he'll need ta catch a seven-foot muskie ta feed all us hungry fellas."

Chapter Eleven

CHASING OLD JACK

Sergeant Curtis stared out between the slats of a moving boxcar. He sat wedged in by his squad, and he looked about as happy as a shedding rattler. Tobacco juice dribbled from the corner of his mouth, and there was no place to spit it. Finally, in a fit of frustration, he barked, "I wish the gol-dang generals would make up their minds."

"Yeah," sighed Frank. "One minute we's tearin' down the road ta Richmond, an' the next we's stompin' back ta Catlett's Station an' gettin' prodded inta this here crowded car."

"But we're the lucky ones," reminded Jimmy. "General Bayard's cavalry had to ride their horses where we're going. I saw them racing north while we were getting aboard this train. They're going to be exhausted before any new action begins."

"I don't care where we're goin'," said Bucky, "as long as we're movin' instead o' settin' 'round some camp."

"Wherever we's headin'," assured Boone, "you kin bet there's some fightin' involved. I know 'cause my trigger finger's been itchin' ever since we left Catlett's Station."

Bucky and his squad rode the train all night, and when they looked outside the next morning, they found the terrain had changed from rolling Virginia farmland to misty blue mountains. When the engine chugged through a pass in this

94

range, Bucky could see a broad valley ahead that was divided down the center by yet another mountain. Finally, the train coasted down a long slope and pulled up at a station bearing the sign "Front Royal."

"Where did they get the name for this burg?" wondered Jimmy aloud after he climbed down from the boxcar and glanced up the little village's only street.

"Why, it's in front o' the mountain that splits this here valley in two," chuckled Boone, "an' it sure is a royal place compared ta that stinkin' flatlander paradise called Camp Pierpont."

"Looks a lot like home ta me," said Bucky. "Them hills is loaded with hemlocks an' cedars."

"I hope the huntin's as good here," added Frank. "I'd like nothin' better than ta bag my limit o' Rebs."

"W-W-Where are w-w-we?" stammered Scarecrow. "S-S-Still in Virginia?"

"Welcome ta the Shenandoah Valley, sonny boy," replied Sergeant Curtis, spitting tobacco juice onto the train station platform. "This here is Stonewall Jackson land, an' he eats timid fellas fer breakfast. Better have yer brave face on, Scarecrow, er you're gonna be the first one Old Jack con-sumes."

The Bucktails paced about the station the rest of the afternoon, swapping gossip and gawking at their new surroundings. At the far end of town was a railroad bridge that spanned a broad river. Beyond that, little farms and woodlots dotted the countryside. To the extreme west, the valley was hemmed in by another series of high blue mountains.

When Bayard's cavalry still had not appeared at dusk, the soldiers lay down wherever they could find room and dozed restlessly until dawn. By order of Lieutenant Colonel Kane, they carried no blankets or tents, so they woke shivering to the damp morning air. They had no breakfast, either, for they had received no rations since weevil-ridden hardtack and tough salt pork were passed out at Catlett's Station.

"I don't mind travelin' light," stewed Sergeant Curtis, "but at least they coulda give us some coffee ta brew."

"You mean Irish coffee, don't ya?" asked Boone with a smirk. "But I know. Them generals don't allow us no whiskey."

"I wouldn't want no whiskey anyhow," added Dan Lemon. "Look at what happened ta Comfort an' Miles when they took a little nip."

"But that was laudanum they drank," corrected Jimmy.

"Tell them that, buried the way they is."

Bucky and his squad milled about the station until noon. They still received no orders from their officers, who seemed as puzzled and jittery as the enlisted men. Bucky saw Lieutenant Colonel Kane pacing back and forth like a caged rooster waiting for a chicken fight. Every half-hour or so, Kane disappeared into the telegraph office and then returned to pace and mutter, mutter and pace.

To keep himself occupied, Jimmy began counting bucktailed hats to see how many riflemen had made this trip. After a half-hour he said, "Two hundred sixty-four."

"What are you babblin' about?" asked Sergeant Curtis.

"Two hundred sixty-four. That's the strength of our fighting force," replied Jimmy. "That includes everybody from Companies C, G, H, and I."

"T-T-That d-d-don't s-s-seem like enough fellas to f-f-fight a w-w-whole R-R-Reb army," stuttered Scarecrow. "'S-S-Specially one r-r-run by S-S-Stonewall J-J-Jackson."

"Hey, it ain't the number o' men that counts. It's what they got in here," said Bucky, thumping the left side of his chest.

When the sun began its descent toward the mountains at the far side of the valley, General Bayard and his cavalry galloped up the railroad grade in a cloud of red dust.

"Why are your troops standing around?" shouted the general to Lieutenant Colonel Kane. "Form 'em up. We've got Stonewall Jackson's wagon train to catch."

The Bucktails rushed into marching formation and double-timed it after the Flying Brigade, which bolted down the railroad grade toward Strasburg. The riflemen covered nine miles before they caught up with Bayard's troops watering their horses in the North Fork of the Shenandoah River. There, Kane hurried forward and began an animated conversation with Bayard.

To Bucky, the two officers looked like turkey gobblers squaring off over a hen. He straggled toward the river to fill his canteen, hoping to catch snatches of their powwow.

"What do you mean that Old Jack slipped out of the trap?" asked Kane in disbelief.

"I received a dispatch just before arriving at Front Royal," replied the general, "and it said Jackson's army is in Strasburg. Somehow that rascal knew Fremont was coming from the west and us from the east to cut him off from his little foray to Harper's Ferry. Some of Old Jack's force have already passed below Massanutten Mountain and are moving posthaste down the turnpike toward Harrisonburg."

"He must have dang good spies to have learned of our plan," said the lieutenant colonel. "What should we do now?"

"Apparently, Jackson's supply train is still behind the rest of the army, and General McDowell has ordered us to destroy it. There should only be a few Rebel cavalry to run off. We have orders to burn every wagon we can lay our hands on."

"Let's get after them, General."

"Thomas, we'd better proceed carefully from here though. Send out a skirmish line of your best men, and the rest of us will follow at a safe distance to stay out of any trap that Jackson might have laid for us. Remember, Thomas, go cautiously."

"Yes, sir," Kane said.

Grinning at the news, Bucky dipped his canteen full of water and scurried back into line just as Lieutenant Colonel Kane was ordering Curtis' squad forward with some select men from Cameron County. The skirmishers fanned out and moved along the railroad grade toward Strasburg, peering into each ditch and clump of brush that might conceal a Confederate sniper. Finally, the Bucktails spied a bridge that they approached in battle formation until Sergeant Curtis motioned for them to take cover.

From his position behind a pile of broken railroad ties, Curtis could see what appeared to be two field pieces and a skeleton crew of Reb gunners protected by a breastwork stretching across the tracks in front of the bridge. To confirm his suspicions, the sergeant waved for Bucky, Boone, and Lemon to scramble to his side.

"What do you fellas see up the tracks there?" Curtis asked after his men had joined him.

"Looks like Old Jack has pre-pared a hot welcome fer us," observed Boone.

"Must be they's fixin' ta destroy the bridge ta keep us from catchin' their wagons," added Lemon. "Them cannon loaded with grapeshot could easily hold us off 'til they put the torch ta her."

"Yeah, what's the loss o' two cannon compared ta their whole wagon train?" agreed Boone.

"I don't know, Sergeant," objected Bucky. "There's somethin' 'bout them field pieces that don't look right. The cannon on the left has a crook in the barrel that shouldn't be there."

"Now that you mention it," said Curtis, "that one does look kinda odd. But maybe the shadows is makin' the cannon barrel appear that way."

"There's only one way ta find out, Sergeant. Bein' we don't have a spyglass, we'll jess have ta git closer fer a better look-see."

"What are you waitin' fer, Culp? You an' Boone git goin'. If ya sneak along the side o' the railroad grade, ya should be safe from their snipers."

"Okay," replied Bucky, "but could ya have Dan take a potshot at any Rebs that start movin' toward us while we're down below? That way we'll have some warnin' while we're movin' along blind."

"You're always thinkin' ahead, ain't ya, Culp?" said Curtis with a grin.

"Yeah, Bucky, keep it up, an' you'll be wearin' corporal's stripes before ya know it," kidded Boone.

"Good luck, boys, an' stay low," warned the sergeant.

Bucky and Boone slid to the bottom of the railroad embankment and then slipped along noiselessly until they were within a hundred yards of the bridge pilings. They couldn't see what the enemy was doing above them, and Bucky could feel the sweat running down his back as they crept even closer. Finally, when they had closed to seventy-five yards, he tapped Boone on the shoulder and pointed to the top of the grade. Slowly, they wormed upward until they could peek over the bank. Taking off their hats, they exposed just their heads while checking out the enemy gun emplacement.

Bucky was the first to spy the ruse, and he groaned to Boone, "Lookee there. Old Jack tricked us with logs, black paint, an' busted wagon wheels."

"Them's called Quaker guns," chuckled Boone. "An' them straw men sure would keep the crows outta any cornfield."

"I don't see nothin' ta laugh at," snapped Bucky, wiping the nervous sweat from his brow. "Them Rebs jess bought some valuable time, an' that wagon train is gittin' farther away every minute."

"Sorry, Bucky. You're right. Let's signal the sergeant an' git movin'."

Bucky and Boone leaped up and waved to Curtis' skirmishers. Then they hurried boldly past the dummy cannons and climbed onto the bridge railing to peer into the distance. When they saw Old Jack's wagon train passing through the village just ahead, they windmilled their arms excitedly to get their unit to hurry.

Finally, after what seemed like an hour, Sergeant Curtis and the rest of the Bucktails charged onto the bridge, and Bucky babbled excitedly, "Old Jack's train is jess ahead. Let's go, boys. Come on."

With Bucky in the lead, the skirmishers pressed forward with renewed vigor and a bit of recklessness. Jimmy and Boone were also loping forward well ahead of the advancing Union line when Confederate batteries began raining shells from the heights above Strasburg. Bucky and his mates hit the dirt when a round exploded in a hot orange fireball not more than fifty yards in front of them. This was followed by an even closer explosion that sent bits of shrapnel whining over the Bucktails' heads. The Rebel fire became so hot that General Bayard galloped forward and ordered his men to retreat beyond the range of the enemy's howitzers. No one was hurt in the shelling, but the men's faces were much paler than they had been at the beginning of the operation.

"Them cannons was like big bulldogs that barked an' howled like they wanted ta bite us," said Frank, after the blood returned to his face.

"An' from what I could see," chuckled Boone, "Old Jack keeps 'em on a strict diet o' blue-bellied soldiers."

When darkness fell, General Bayard withdrew his Flying Brigade to the eastern side of the Shenandoah River after ordering the Bucktails to guard the railroad bridge. Curtis' squad stayed on the Strasburg side while the rest of the riflemen bivouacked at the other end of the bridge next to the cavalry.

The June night was not unpleasant, so the Bucktails didn't miss their blankets like they had at Front Royal. Their stomachs still grumbled, though, until a Union supply wagon emerged from the gloom, and a ration of coffee and a half ration of hardtack was passed out to each of the famished men.

"Jess like the gol-dang army," complained Curtis while he crunched on a petrified biscuit. "They finally got 'round ta givin' us coffee when we ain't allowed ta light no fires."

"W-W-Why c-c-can't w-w-we have a f-f-fire, Sergeant?" asked Scarecrow.

"We don't wanna give away our position ta the Rebs, do we? If their rear guard knew exactly where we was, they'd come sneakin' across that field an' . . . cut out yer gizzard like this."

Curtis grabbed Scarecrow and planted his thumb in the boy's belly button. Then the sergeant ran his thumb upward in knifelike imitation to Sam's chest. Scarecrow wheezed and turned white. His eyes welled up with tears, and he flailed madly with his arms and legs to free himself from Curtis' grip. The more he struggled, the tighter his antagonist held him. It wasn't until a wet spot appeared on the front of Scarecrow's pants that Curtis finally released him.

When the sergeant laughed cruelly, Jimmy growled, "What's with you, Hosea? How's Sam supposed to get any confidence if his own squad tries to scare him half to death? We don't want him to freeze up in battle, do we? That might cost all of us our lives."

"Yeah, Sergeant, lay off the kid," urged Dan Lemon. "I think we should try an' figger out how ta catch that Reb supply train. That's the only way we's gonna git anything good ta eat."

"An' we'd have a nice fire ta cook it over, too," snickered Boone, "once we put the torch ta them wagons."

The night passed quickly for the Bucktails, who took turns sleeping and standing watch. Bucky and Jimmy drew the last watch, and they marveled at the beauty of the misty blue mountains that took shape with the first glimmer of daylight.

"This kinda reminds me o' the night I spent at yer house before we enlisted," whispered Bucky, with a dreamy look in his eye. "Before dawn I set in a chair by yer bedroom window an' watched the trees appear outta the darkness as by shaman magic."

"Yeah, I remember sleeping outside that night after the terrible fight I had with Mother. I was a real baby, wasn't I?"

"No, I think you was jess a fella with somethin' ta prove ta himself. Kinda like Scarecrow."

"I'm glad Mother understood . . . later. I guess she's even a little bit proud of me now."

"She should be—"

The friends' whispers were interrupted by the tramp of the rest of the regiment streaming across the bridge. Lieutenant Colonel Kane was in the lead, and he barked, "Fall in, men. We've been ordered to reconnoiter Strasburg."

Bucky and Jimmy slipped into line, and the Bucktails crept cautiously up the railroad tracks before fanning into a battle line at the outskirts of the little village. They moved from tree to tree and house to house until they discovered the Rebs had evacuated, leaving behind smoldering fires, discarded equipment, and broken wagons.

Word was sent back to the Flying Brigade, and General Bayard's men came clattering into town moments later. They were followed soon after by several batteries of General Fremont's mountain howitzers that had finally arrived from the west. When Fremont's infantry came straggling in last, Bucky figured that they must have marched most of the night by the way they bowed beneath the weight of their packs. The ranks were silent, too, and many of the soldiers' eyes kept closing as they walked woodenly along.

"Look at them heavy-loaded fellas," chuckled Boone. "What have they got in them packs—anvils or pi-anos?"

"Yeah, how do they expect ta keep up with Old Jack carryin' all that gear?" wondered Sergeant Curtis. "I'm glad I'm a rifleman when I see how Fremont's infantry boys are draggin'."

The Bucktails didn't have long to gloat, however, before they were ordered forward in pursuit of Jackson's retreating army. Much of the time they trotted to keep up with Bayard's cavalry. It was a grueling pace even for woodsmen and ridge runners, and Bucky, Frank, and Boone were short of breath after a couple of hours.

Around ten in the morning the Bucktails made their first contact with the Confederate rear guard that burst out of a thicket in a fierce attack. The charge was led by Reb cavalry and was so sudden that Bucky and his squad only had time to fire one volley before the enemy forces were nose to nose with them. The Bucktails used their muskets as clubs to fend off the horsemen until a counterattack by Bayard's 1st New Jersey Cavalry repulsed the Rebs and forced them back into the bush.

"Was that ever close," said Frank, whistling with relief.

"We was lucky, all right," agreed Sergeant Curtis before growling to Scarecrow, "You kin pick yer jaw off the ground. They's gone."

"Weren't those Rebels Ashby's Black Horse Cavalry?" asked Jimmy, also visibly shaken.

"I thought I recognized them fellas," said Frank. "You should remember 'em, too, Boone, after them battles around New Creek last fall."

"All I remember is that I'da blown old Turner Ashby outta the saddle if Kane hadn't stopped me."

"I remember now," said Bucky. "We was on patrol, an' General Ashby rode right by us, not knowin' we was there."

"I coulda picked 'im off blindfolded," sighed Boone, "but Kane knocked my gun away an' said that Ashby was too brave ta die that way."

"You have to realize," said Jimmy, "that a lot of these Union and Rebel officers knew each other before the war and still are good friends. Some of them even fought together in the Mexican War. There's a code of honor between them because they're gentlemen."

"As if we ain't," said Frank with mock seriousness. "I'm so insulted, I'm gonna have ta snipe me a Reb officer jess ta cool off."

The Bucktails again pressed forward with Bayard's cavalry, but as the afternoon wore on, they had more and more difficulty keeping up with the horsemen. By five o'clock a steady rain began to fall, and the chase was mercifully called off after the Flying Brigade occupied the town of Woodstock. Fremont's infantry was still well behind. They didn't trudge into camp until Bucky and his squad were boiling coffee over a low fire they had built behind some shielding rocks.

The conversation sputtered quickly after dinner. Bucky's squad sought shelter in a grove of hemlocks and fell instantly into an exhausted sleep. Only Scarecrow stayed awake. He sat with his back against a tree, staring bug-eyed into the gloom. His only weapon was a drummer's short sword. Whimpering, he thrust it at every intruding shadow.

The chase was on again at seven the next morning when the Bucktails formed a skirmish line and pushed forward with Bayard's 1st Pennsylvania Cavalry. The Rebs were like ghosts, though, and they melted into the misty woods each time they fired a few diversionary rounds. Despite the wet weather and Rebel ambushes, the Flying Brigade's pursuit was swift until it reached Edinburg. There, a superior force of Reb infantry held the Union cavalry and the Bucktails at bay with volley after volley until they torched the Stony Creek Bridge.

When the bridge burst into flame, Bucky groaned, "Dang, there was too many o' 'em ta drive off."

"Yeah," growled Curtis, "that gol-dang Reb regiment jess bought Jackson a few more hours ta make his escape."

Stony Creek was swollen with rain, and Bucky's squad was sent to find a suitable ford for Fremont's infantry and artillery. They had gone only a couple hundred yards upstream when the crack of muskets had them ducking for cover. Bucky dove behind a bent hemlock while Sergeant Curtis, Boone, Frank, and Jimmy slid flat on their bellies to get behind a clump of rocks.

"Bucky, did ya see where them Rebs is shootin' from?" called Curtis.

"No, Sergeant. All I know is that they's above us."

"Well, someone's gonna have ta draw their fire, er we'll be pinned down here a long time."

"I'll go," said Jimmy, and he leaped up and sprinted ahead dodging between the trees. The Reb snipers fired another volley, and Jimmy toppled forward, disappearing from his squad's view.

"Jimmy. Jimmy. Are you all right?" shouted Bucky, peering around the hemlock trunk.

"I . . . I . . . I think so. I slipped on some moss just as those Rebels starting shooting. I fell pretty hard. I wasn't hit, though."

"Them Rebs is denned up like a bunch of rattlers on that rocky ledge jess ta the right," hissed Frank. "I saw their muzzle flashes when they blasted at Jimmy. They's well protected. How kin we root 'em out o' there?"

"There's one of them rascals," whispered Boone. "Right in that openin' in them rocks. I'll show you fellas how to git 'im."

The enemy sniper was barely visible in a narrow crevice less than half the width of the man's head. Sergeant Curtis and Frank guffawed at their comrade's boast while Boone aimed along his rifle barrel and squeezed off a deliberate shot. A cry echoed from above, and the rest of the Rebel snipers scrambled from hiding and scattered for higher ground. The crack of Bucktail muskets rang out again, and three more Rebels fell dead. Before Bucky, Frank, and Curtis could reload, the rest of the Confederates melted into the highlands and were seen no more.

When the Bucktails climbed to the ledge above, they found the Reb that Boone had killed. Boone's bullet had dead-centered the sniper in the forehead, and a look of pure surprise was frozen on the corpse's ashen face.

"How in the devil did you do that?" asked Jimmy in awe. "I couldn't even see the bugger myself, let alone get a shot at him."

"Concentration is what it was," crowed Boone. "Pure an' simple. An' a trigger squeeze smooth as a baby's behind. I was born with a Kentuck rifle in my hands an' could shoot the eye out of a roostin' turkey be-fore I took my first step."

"If I hadn't seen it with my own eyes," groaned Sergeant Curtis, "I'da thought it was jess another of yer gol-dang tall tales, Boone."

"It will be before he's through braggin'," said Bucky. "The next time we hear the story, he'll have shot that Reb through solid rock."

After locating the other three dead Rebs, Curtis led his squad back to Stony Creek. They encountered no more enemy fire while they found a suitable crossing place for Fremont's army. This sergeant, Bucky, and Jimmy stayed to secure the ford while Boone and Frank returned to fetch the Union forces. Bayard's cavalry arrived first, followed by the infantry and a battery of mountain howitzers. By noon, the whole Federal army was safely across the swollen stream, and Curtis' squad received a congratulatory salute from General Fremont, who galloped to and fro prodding his troop to hurry.

With no time to stop for lunch and no food to feed them, the Bucktails and the Flying Brigade rushed off once more to harass the Rebels' retreat. Hour after hour the riflemen's brutal fatigue march kept pace with the horsemen. Whenever a nest of Reb snipers tried ambushing the cavalry, there were the Bucktails and their pinpoint shooting to foil the enemy's trap.

After Curtis' squad had smoked out a particularly pesky group of Rebs, Bucky overheard a 1st New Jersey trooper exclaim, "How do them Bucktails shoot so accurate after all them miles they marched? I'd be too tired to hold up a dang musket, let alone hit somethin' with it."

"I know what ya mean," replied another cavalryman. "If I double-timed it fer ten miles like they done, I wouldn't be able to hit a bull in the be-hind with a snow shovel."

Toward evening Bayard's force charged through the little village of Mt. Jackson and drove off a clump of Confederates that were attempting to set fire to the Cedar Mill Creek Bridge. Bucky blew the torch from one Reb's hands while Boone and Frank shot two other saboteurs attempting to burn the bridge pilings on the far side of the creek. After Jimmy and Curtis squeezed off equally deadly shots that left two more quivering corpses lying in the road, the remaining Rebs skedaddled.

Curtis' squad had little time to celebrate their success, however, before Bucky spotted smoke rising in the distance from the more strategic bridge over the North Fork of the Shenandoah River. When Bucky and Jimmy arrived at the river's edge, the bridge collapsed in a shower of sparks into the swift-moving current. A unit of Confederate cavalry was on the opposite bank, and the troopers paused long enough to give a sarcastic salute before dashing away in a whirlwind of taunting laughter.

"Dang," said Bucky, as the Rebs galloped off, "that one horseman looked jess like Jeb Starr. He had the scrawny build, the same weasely face, an' everything. He even laughed like 'im."

"You know, I thought the same thing," agreed Jimmy. "Maybe fatigue is playing tricks on us because we both know that's impossible."

"What's impossible?" asked Boone. "Are you boys still talkin' 'bout that shot I made back yonder?"

"The only thing impossible about that is you not braggin' 'bout it," taunted Frank. "Hey, have any of you boys seen Dan Lemon lately?"

"He dropped out of line a couple of miles back," replied Jimmy. "Said he had a sore foot."

"Him an' about half the other fellas that started this here march," grunted Curtis. "Us Bucktails is down ta a hundred an' fifty men er so. I guess keepin' pace with cavalry ain't so easy after all."

"Yeah, b-b-but I m-m-made it," stammered Sam proudly. "You d-d-didn't figure I w-w-would, d-d-did you, S-S-Sergeant?"

"Ya done good, Scarecrow," said Curtis, fighting back a grin. "Now we gotta get ya over yer fear o' Rebs. Remember, they walks on two legs jess like us. I guess you're the last recruit ta make it now that Lemon's dropped out. Ya must be tougher than ya look by a long shot."

The rest of the squad gave Scarecrow congratulatory pats on the back, and then they were called to help construct a pontoon bridge to replace the one that had been destroyed by the Rebs. Sergeant Curtis, a former lumberman, was put in charge of the operation, and he barked out orders and cursed at those who didn't follow them. They worked all night to complete the floating structure and about had it tied in place when a sudden rise in the river forced Curtis' crew to cut the ropes and let the bridge swing to the northern shore.

It wasn't until ten o'clock the next morning that the North Fork of the Shenandoah went down enough to permit the bridge to be swung across the current and secured. While the Bucktails scampered over to the south bank to join Bayard's cavalry, Jimmy said, "Now, it looks like we're really going to have to move. Jackson's army has an eighteen-hour lead on us."

The Bucktails were famous skirmishers and sharpshooters. At the Battle of Harrisonburg they fought Indian-style, firing from behind trees at the superior Reb forces.

The troops were most vulnerable when they were reloading their muskets during a battle. Soldiers had to stand or kneel to ram home another ball. This movement often gave away their positions to enemy snipers. Many hand and arm wounds resulted.

Chapter Twelve

SCARECROW'S BATTLE

The Bucktail skirmishers and the Flying Brigade pressed forward for another day and a half without making further contact with Stonewall Jackson's retreating forces. By the time the troops reached the village of Harrisonburg in the afternoon of June sixth, the riflemen were on the verge of exhaustion from their grueling fatigue march. Fremont was still eager to locate the Rebs, so General Bayard's 1st New Jersey Cavalry was sent on alone without Bucktail scouts. The general also remained behind in Harrisonburg with his worn-out 1st Pennsylvania troopers.

Bucky, Jimmy, Scarecrow, and the rest of their squad literally fell out of rank when they were dismissed in Harrisonburg. They lay motionless under a shade tree for some time before Frank said, "How many miles do you fellas think we marched since crossin' the Shenandoah River?"

"Upwards ta forty," groused Sergeant Curtis, "if my throbbin' feet are any indication. How far do you think we come, Boone?"

"Don't know . . . an' I don't care. I need a good snooze 'cause my brain's even tireder than my legs. Look at Scarecrow. He's already sawin' logs. I hope ta join him right quick."

"Boy, we musta come a long way," said Bucky, "if Boone's run outta things ta joke about."

"Amen to that," added Jimmy. "I hope we don't catch General Jackson until we get a good rest. By my count, our regiment is down to 104 men—who can still walk."

The Bucktails napped in the shade until the unmistakable pop of distant musket fire disturbed their slumber. When the firing became more intense, officers circulated to each group of dozing men and ordered them to their feet. Bucky stood up and wobbled groggily into formation. Scarecrow, however, could not be roused, so Jimmy and Frank hoisted up the drummer boy by the armpits and dragged him still snoozing into line next to a dazed Boone.

Lieutenant Colonel Kane stood in the road with Captain Blanchard, Captain Taylor, and Captain McDonald, listening to the distant battle. They were joined by General Bayard when a squad of disheveled cavalry galloped into Harrisonburg in full retreat.

"What's going on out there?" snapped the general after the horsemen reined to a halt and gave hurried salutes.

"We got ourselves ambushed by Ashby's boys," said a flustered sergeant. "They hit us from the front an' both flanks. A massacre is what it is, sir. Our colors was captured an' Colonel Wyndham wounded. There was wounded lying everywhere when we . . . got ordered back . . . to bring the news."

"Are you sure you were sent back, soldier, or just run off on your own? I'll have your hide if I find out it's the latter. Join up with the 1st Pennsylvania Cavalry. I'll deal with you and your men later."

After the cavalrymen had cantered sheepishly away, Kane said to Bayard, "Sir, we can't leave poor Wyndham on the field with our wounded. Let my riflemen go forward to assist them."

"Do you think that's wise, Colonel? The Rebel rear guard seems to be of considerable force if what the sergeant said is even half true."

"We won't know unless we send somebody out there to verify his report. Besides, General, think how such a stampede as this will dishearten and demoralize the men. Let me at those Rebs with my Bucktails."

"Just forty minutes I'll give you, Colonel," said Bayard, pulling out his watch. "Scout these woods on our left, see what's in there, and come back again when time's up."

With the 1st Pennsylvania Cavalry protecting his right flank, Lieutenant Colonel Kane led his Bucktails into the woods Bayard asked him to reconnoiter. Sergeant Curtis' squad was positioned next to the cavalry, and they slunk along, peering into the brush ahead. Bucky and Boone were on point, and they had gone about a mile or so when the boom of a concealed battery had them diving for cover. The cannon balls fell to their right, however, and Bucky watched fountains of earth explode in the midst of the horsemen. The Reb battery poured shell after shell into the cavalry formation, blowing over many mounts and stampeding others. Finally, the 1st Pennsylvania regiment was forced to gallop back toward Harrisonburg to escape the deadly bombardment that had fallen like hail among them.

"Dang," said Bucky. "If they hadn't run fer it, they'da been butchered sure as them Jersey boys."

"I'm jess glad them Rebs weren't firin' on us," replied a very pale Boone. "I'll take all the bullets they wanna shoot at me, but there's somethin' 'bout them cannon projectiles that give me the creeps."

"All right, Bucktails, the barrage is over," snarled Colonel Kane. "What are you cowering behind those trees for? Move out. That means you, too, Culp. Crossmire."

Red-faced, Bucky and Boone got to their feet and moved slowly forward, dodging from tree to tree. Because it was now getting toward evening, Bucky couldn't help but think how the lengthening shadows provided perfect cover for the gray-coated enemy. His nerves tensed with each step he took farther into Reb territory. By the time Bucky had gone two more miles, he was sure his heartbeat could be heard fifty yards in any direction.

Bucky moved even more cautiously as he slipped along toward a glen that opened up directly in front of him. It was a good thing he was vigilant because it was there that a full regiment of Rebel infantry came charging from cover and opened up on the Bucktail skirmish line. The bullets were so thick in the air around Bucky that only the tree he had stopped behind saved him from sure death.

After the thunder of the initial Rebel volley had died away, Bucky and his comrades began firing from behind trees Indian-style. They shot with such murderous precision that within minutes they collapsed the center of the Confederate line.

"That'll fix 'em," shouted Sergeant Curtis when he saw the Rebels fall back. "Is that all the esteemed 58th Virginia's got? They don't de-serve that fancy flag they're flyin'."

Not knowing that most of the Rebel regiment was hidden by the crest of a hill, Lieutenant Colonel Kane rose to signal for an attack. Before he could give the command, Private Martin Kelly of Company G shouted, "Shall I draw their fire?" With that, he stepped from behind a tree and was blown backward by a volley of balls shot by the concealed Confederates.

Kane gasped when he saw the extent of the Rebel force and said to Captain Taylor, "We would have committed certain suicide if not for that brave fellow. Now I can see how outnumbered we are. Let's give 'em hell until Fremont sends reinforcements."

The words were barely out of Kane's mouth before the Confederate commander, General Turner Ashby, rode to the front of the Rebel line and fired a pistol at his Union counterpart. The bullet pierced Kane's leg, and he writhed in pain and collapsed heavily against a tree. Then Boone, Frank, and Bucky leveled their rifles at Ashby and fired a deadly volley that downed the general's mount.

"We didn't spare yer lousy hide at New Creek so ya could wound our colonel," screamed an enraged Boone. "Take that, Ashby."

While Ashby was rolling free from his dead horse, Lieutenant Colonel Kane righted himself and spotted a group of Confederates charging across a little glen to outflank his Bucktails. "Curtis!" Kane cried in a raspy voice. "To the left. Take your men to the left."

Sergeant Curtis placed his squad in position to defend the left side of the Bucktail line, and they fired with such accuracy that the Rebels began to fall back once more. Cursing, Ashby crawled to his feet and howled above the battle din, "Virginians! Fix bayonets! Charge!" The general drew his sword and took one step before a Bucktail corporal, who was lying mortally wounded at Kane's feet, rose up on one elbow and shot Ashby square in the chest, killing him instantly.

A cheer rose from the Bucktails' ranks, and Curtis shouted, "That's all fer Ashby, that gol-dang scoundrel. Keep firin', men."

After edging closer to Kane to protect their wounded leader, Jimmy and Bucky furiously reloaded their muskets and blasted the faltering Rebel ranks. Both soldiers' faces were black with powder smoke, and their eyes had a steely glint. All around them lay their dead and wounded comrades, nearly fifty in all.

Scarecrow also was down, but not because he was hit. He lay curled up in a ball at the base of a tree, too frightened to defend himself or even move.

"Git up, Scarecrow," bellowed Sergeant Curtis to the unresponsive drummer, "before I drag ya up by the ears."

"Leave him alone, Sergeant," barked Jimmy. "Can't you see he's petrified?"

"Guess he shoulda stayed home with Mama."

Lieutenant Colonel Kane, meanwhile, watched the Rebels mill about bewailing the death of General Ashby. He, too, felt sad about losing his old friend. They had frequented the same social circles before the war, and Kane knew him to be a fine gentleman and valiant officer. Kane didn't blame Ashby for his wounded leg because in battle it was a soldier's duty to kill opposing officers first. If the officers were all dead, the cowards would run away and take the brave men with them. Not that the Bucktails had any cowards.

Kane's reverie was broken by a searing pain that ripped through his chest. He was struck by a Minie ball, and he slid to the ground, faint from shock and the loss of blood. He slipped in and out of consciousness until he heard one of his lieutenants whisper in his ear, "Shall I get some men to carry you back, Colonel? It's best if we retreat before we're all captured."

"No, Lieutenant," said Kane doggedly. "You are doing nobly. Give them hell."

Bucky grinned at Kane's words and continued his manic firing and reloading. In front of him he could see another contingent of Rebels scurrying forward, waving the 1st Maryland banner. He trained his sights on the colorbearer and squeezed a true shot that sent the man skidding on his face. Another soldier picked up the flag, and Boone dropped him before he had gone two steps. This seemed to anger the Rebels as much as the loss of General Ashby, and they rushed the Bucktails with renewed fury until they were within a hundred fifty feet of Bucky's position.

In spite of the Bucktails' precise shooting, a squad of the 1st Maryland infantry broke through the Union line just as Kane attempted to sit up. A tall, rawboned Reb private slammed his rifle butt into Kane's sternum, knocking him senseless. Next, the Reb turned on Scarecrow, where he lay looking up with pleading eyes, and rammed his bayonet through the drummer boy's side. Captain Blanchard charged the private but was shot by a sniper through both legs before he could wield his sword. Blanchard lay defenselessly squirming at the mercy of the brutal Reb, who raised his now reloaded musket to snuff out the captain's life. Before the enemy's finger tightened on the trigger, a snarling Sergeant Curtis leaped on the man from behind. Curtis wrenched the musket from the rawboned Reb and broke the Confederate soldier's jaw with a vicious thrust of the rifle butt. The sergeant continued to smash at the Rebel's face long after he was dead. "Gol-dang you," Curtis wailed, "Scarecrow never hurt nobody. Nobody. Nobody!"

Curtis' frenzy continued until Captain Taylor barked, "Sergeant, forget him. Help me with Kane. Sergeant!"

Curtis snarled again at the dead man and broke the Reb's musket over his knee. Snatching up his own empty rifle, he joined Taylor at Kane's side. The lieutenant colonel was moaning softly and was so woozy from the loss of blood that he could barely raise his head. Finally, he muttered with extreme effort, "Looks like Fremont isn't coming, Captain . . . It's almost dark. We fought a game fight, but it's time to . . . retreat. Go now. Save what's left of the men, Captain. Half of them are already . . . down."

"But what about you, sir?"

"You'll never get away lugging me. Go now. That's an order."

Captain Taylor saluted his brave commander, shouted for the survivors to follow him, and then rushed off at a dead run north through the darkening woods. Frank and Boone were close at the captain's heels, but Bucky and Jimmy stopped to attend to Scarecrow, who was now barely breathing. Blood gushed from his lacerated side, and Jimmy held a handkerchief over the wound to try to slow the bleeding. The drummer was too weak to answer when Jimmy called, "Sam. Sam. Can you hear me?"

Sergeant Curtis lagged behind because he saw several Maryland soldiers rip a bucktail from a wounded man's hat and tie it to their flagpole for a trophy. Cursing, Curtis reloaded his musket, took careful aim, and fired into the enemy huddle.

"Gol-dang Rebs, anyhow," grunted Curtis when he saw two Confederates fall dead to the ground. "They ain't gonna make no mockery of us Bucktails long as I'm standin'."

"Come on, Sergeant. It's time ta go," shouted Bucky. "More Rebs is comin', an' they's comin' fast."

After warning Curtis, Bucky handed his musket to Jimmy, slung Sam over his shoulder, and ran like he'd never run before. Bucky could hear Jimmy crashing along behind him as he dodged trees like a bat and hit the open field beyond the forest in full stride.

Sergeant Curtis reluctantly followed when a wave of Maryland infantry surged toward him through the dusk. The sergeant was a big man, built more for brawling than running, but with the bullets singing past his ear, he knew it was time to take to his legs. Rumbling along like a retreating bear, he careened through the woods and then loped across an open field. He caught Bucky and Jimmy just as they reached a chest-high fence that separated the field from another woodlot.

Jimmy was the first one over the barrier. Bucky and Curtis carefully hoisted Scarecrow over the rails to him. Bucky climbed over next while Curtis turned and fired at a group of charging Rebels that was closing fast. Bucky and Jimmy shot to cover their sergeant, but their volley did little to discourage the persistent Rebs. Before Curtis scrambled over the fence after his comrades, the Maryland infantry had closed to within five rods of him.

On the other side of the fence, the Bucktails bolted until their mouths tasted of copper. Bucky was oblivious to Scarecrow's weight. Nor did he feel the drummer boy's blood soaking through his jacket. Like Jimmy and Curtis, Bucky raced blindly on until the soldiers Captain Taylor had led from the Rebel hornet's nest appeared suddenly on the path ahead.

"Where you boys been?" asked Frank wearily when his friends came tearing from the woods. "We was sure that the Rebs got ya."

"That'll . . . be . . . the day," puffed the out-of-breath Curtis. "Us Bucktails can outfight . . . outshoot . . . an' outsmart . . . any gol-dang Reb . . . in-cludin' . . . Old Jack . . . hisself."

"Don't forgit 'outrun' from that list of yers," chuckled Boone.

"Hey, I don't think we done . . . so gol-dang bad . . . considerin' we was outnumbered . . . five to one," wheezed the sergeant. "They mighta drove us off . . . but we made 'em pay a heavy price . . . Why, there was Reb bodies lyin' everywhere . . . An' don't forgit General Ashby . . . We picked 'im off like a pigeon."

"What about Scarecrow?" asked Frank. "How's he doin', Bucky?"

"Not so good, Frank. He ain't moved much in the last mile I toted him. I hope he makes it."

"We'll take him straight to the hospital when we get to Harrisonburg," said Jimmy. "Pray that the Lord is merciful."

"Look. There's the town jess ahead," shouted Boone. "We made it!"

Taylor's Bucktails straggled into Harrisonburg and found a pacing General Bayard waiting to greet them. "Captain, why didn't Lieutenant Colonel Kane return in forty minutes like he was instructed?" demanded the general, looking with despair at the tiny group of survivors.

"We were pinned down by two infantry regiments, sir, and the lieutenant colonel isn't one to back down from any fight."

"Yes, Captain Taylor, but his orders were to scout out the enemy, not engage him."

"Well, sir, the lieutenant colonel stayed put because he believed that General Fremont would send up reinforcements."

"Kane should have known darn well that Fremont couldn't risk an all-out battle until Shields' army arrives from the east side of the Massanutten Mountain. Why isn't the lieutenant colonel here to answer for himself?"

"I fear he is captured, sir. He was shot twice during the engagement and wouldn't let us help him from the field. He thought he'd slow us down, so that none of us would escape."

"And yet you have another wounded man with you. Who is responsible for saving him?"

"Private Culp carried out our drummer, Sam Whalen."

"Good work, Corporal Culp. I need more wildcats like you. I'll have Lieutenant Rice lead you to the field hospital, so your friend can be attended to. Dismissed, men. Get some rest. We're going to need you skirmishers again real soon. I only wish you Bucktails had been with the New Jersey cavalry a few hours ago. I'm sure you'd have kept my boys out of that Rebel trap where Colonel Wyndham was captured. I only hope the impetuous Thomas Kane doesn't meet the same fate."

After the general disappeared into the darkness, Lieutenant Rice said to Bucky, "Come with me, Corporal. The hospital is this way."

"What do ya mean by calling me 'Corporal,' sir?"

"You heard General Bayard. You've been promoted, Culp. Come along now."

Following the lieutenant to the north end of camp, Bucky could feel Scarecrow's body grow stiff on his shoulder. Jimmy had tagged along to lend a hand, and he asked in a worried voice, "Do you think Sam is going to make it? Well, Bucky?"

Bucky didn't answer, and soon the soldiers arrived at the field hospital where they ducked into a lantern-lit surgery tent. Setting Scarecrow down on a straw pallet, they could see it was already too late for their friend. There was no breath leaking from Sam's blue lips, and his eyes were void of light. Even death could not erase the fear he had experienced in battle, for his face was frozen in a grotesque expression of sheer terror.

With all the dying they had seen that day, Bucky and Jimmy were beyond tears. Jimmy reached down and closed Sam's eyelids. Then the preacher's son removed his hat, bowed his head, and prayed in a reverent voice, "Lord, please accept this harmless soul, Samuel Whalen, into Your gracious presence. Look after him, Lord. He was one of Your lost sheep, who has now returned to graze in Your pasture of light. His life was short and full of sorrow. May his reward be everlasting peace."

When an orderly came to tend to Scarecrow's body, Bucky and Jimmy walked stiffly back to the Bucktails' camp. There they found Curtis, Frank, and Boone resting with their backs against a hemlock near a small, inconspicuous fire. By Jimmy's demeanor, the others knew that all had not gone well at the hospital.

"I'm sorry 'bout Scarecrow," said Sergeant Curtis after Bucky and Jimmy collapsed wearily to the ground. "Is he? . . ."

"Yes, he's gone," said Jimmy softly. "To a better place."

"I hope you fellas don't think I enjoyed pickin' on him," continued Curtis in a choked voice. "I was only tryin' ta toughen 'im up before he seen any action."

"Ya only done what my pa done fer me," replied Bucky. "Scarecrow was the weakest pup o' the litter. He had no business bein' in this here war."

After a poignant silence, Frank said, "I hope Lieutenant Colonel Kane is all right. He was hit pretty bad."

"That's why I'm going back to look for him," grunted Captain Taylor from where he rested beneath another tree. "I still can't believe he wouldn't let us save him."

"That's because he was more concerned with our safety than he was for his own," said Jimmy. "If you don't mind, Captain, I'd like to go with you to help find the lieutenant colonel."

"That might not be wise, Private Jewett. You could end up gettin' captured or killed."

"I'm willing to take that risk, sir. If Lieutenant Colonel Kane is still lying on the battlefield, you'll need some help to bring him back."

"I'd better go, too," said Bucky.

"No, if too many of us go," warned Taylor, "the Rebels might think it's a night attack. Then we would risk getting shot. Come along, Jewett. I'll take you, but no one else. It's best that you stay here anyway, Culp."

"Why's that, sir?"

"Because after carrying a wounded comrade three miles, you've displayed enough bravery for one day. I wouldn't be surprised if there's a medal in it for you."

"I'd jess as soon have a cup o' coffee, if it's all the same ta you, Captain."

"Fat chance o' that," grumbled Hosea Curtis. "We got back too late ta git any o' the rations that come up. That's three days in a row we got nothin' ta eat."

"If this keeps up, we'll have ta boil our boots an' eat the leather," said Frank.

"There's always plenty o' cavalry horses around," reminded Boone. "Their steaks is tough, but filling."

"I don't know if I could stomach horse meat," groaned Jimmy.

"Now, Jimmy," smirked Boone. "A starvin' fella can't be picky. An' horse flesh sure'd beat the heck outta filet o' Reb."

"Boone, knock it off," growled Bucky. "We jess got whipped by the Rebs an' lost half our regiment. Kane is missin', an' Scarecrow . . . dead. There's nothin' funny 'bout that."

"That's right, Corporal, you tell him," said Captain Taylor.

"Excuse me, Captain, is the lieutenant colonel kin o' yers?" wondered Hosea. "Is that why you're goin' back ta fetch 'im?"

"No, Sergeant, but General Bayard is my half brother, and the general is one of Thomas Kane's best friends. I know the general would go out looking for Thomas himself if he wasn't under Fremont's strict orders not to do so."

Chapter Thirteen

SEARCHING FOR KANE

Captain Taylor and Jimmy slipped out of Harrisonburg and returned to the wood where the battle had raged a few hours before. A pale moon bathed the forest in an eerie glow, and Jimmy jumped each time the wind rustled the leaves or swayed nearby boughs. Being unarmed intensified Jimmy's nervousness although he realized that bringing his musket only would make it more difficult to carry back their wounded leader once they found him.

The soldiers slunk along as carefully as they could through the gloomy forest. Often they tripped over logs or got entangled in intertwining branches. They wandered in circles a few times, too, before coming to the place where the 1st Pennsylvania Cavalry got bushwhacked by the Reb battery. Here the ground was broken by craters, and dead horses gave off their unmistakable stench. Many trees had been shattered, and broken limbs hung at crazy angles. Although no wounded could be found, two dead troopers lay bathed in moonlight, smashed beneath their stricken mounts.

"I don't know about you, Private Jewett," whispered Taylor, "but I'm tired of wandering around out here in the dark. We found the first battlefield through dumb luck, but we still got at least two more miles to go to find the wood where we fought. If you're in agreement, I think we should light a torch before going any farther."

"But won't we be spotted by the Rebels if we do that?" asked Jimmy with a shiver.

"It's possible, but I think we have to chance it to find the lieutenant colonel."

"T-T-Then we'd better do it," agreed Jimmy.

Captain Taylor found some dry hemlock twigs and tied a bundle of them together with a piece of cloth he ripped from a dead cavalryman's uniform. He daubed the twigs with pitch oozing from a battered tree and lit the completed torch with a match. When the torch sputtered to life, the two soldiers stumbled on, listening to the hooting of owls and the furtive scurry of night creatures through the underbrush.

Finally, Captain Taylor stumbled across the glen where the Confederates had massed for their attack, and he hissed to Jimmy, "Jewett, do you recognize that opening in the trees just ahead? You should because we're entering the wood we held during the battle. Move carefully and keep your eyes open for Lieutenant Colonel Kane."

The captain and Jimmy picked their way across the uneven ground, searching the underbrush and the bases of trees for their missing leader. After a half an hour they identified the bodies of Milton Farr, William Dale, and Corporal Holmes but still had not found Kane.

When they came upon the bullet-riddled form of Martin Kelly, Captain Taylor said, "There'd be a lot more of our boys lying out here if it wasn't for this brave soul. How much starch did it take for him to step out from behind that tree and let the Rebs blow him full of holes?"

"I don't know, sir," replied Jimmy, "but if he hadn't sacrificed himself, we'd have been suckered into their trap for sure."

Captain Taylor began circuiting the wood, looking for the still-missing Kane. He employed the same technique he often used to locate a wounded deer. In the moonlight he made small circles that he expanded outward looking for a blood trail or drag marks that might lead him to his commander. Jimmy, meanwhile, bowed his head to say a silent prayer for the men of both sides who had given up their lives for their convictions.

After an hour, Captain Taylor returned from the underbrush and said, "It looks like the lieutenant colonel must have been captured because he's not anywhere about. Nor is Captain Blanchard. I think I'll give myself up to the Rebs and see if I can find Thomas."

"I'll go, too, sir."

"No, Private Jewett. Now that I'm senior officer of the Bucktails, it's my responsibility. What if we surrender and end up in a prison camp? Do you think you could handle that?"

"Sir, you have to allow me to go," answered Jimmy firmly. "I'm as worried about Colonel Kane as you are, and I know that's what the Lord wants me to do."

"Okay, but let's make another torch before we go on. This one's almost out. If we must go, let's go boldly."

Taylor lit the torch he fashioned from hemlock twigs, and then he and Jimmy started across the Confederate side of the battlefield. As Jimmy followed the captain, he could hear low moans of the unrescued wounded, and he shivered despite the warmth of the June night. He attempted to shuffle closer to Taylor but instead jumped straight in the air when a shadowy hand reached up and grabbed him roughly by the leg. Jimmy cried out and struggled to free himself from the death grip that shackled him. "H-H-Help me," wheezed a phantom voice. "For God's sake help me. Water. Water."

Jimmy cried out again, and Captain Taylor roughly booted the wounded Reb until he let go of Jimmy's leg. The Reb was foaming at the mouth like a rabid dog, and his eyes were blazing with fever. "A curse on all you bluebellies," he gurgled. "A curse on your mothers an' sisters an' cousins an' the whole dang lot of you. Water. Please. Water."

When Jimmy's fright had passed, he took out his canteen to give the delirious man the drink he begged for. Captain Taylor grabbed Jimmy by the arm and said, "Don't go near him. If he has a stomach wound, you'll only make things worse for the poor devil by giving him a drink. After we surrender, we'll tell the Rebs they have more wounded men out here."

Again Captain Taylor led the way south until they reached a dense thicket totally immersed in shadow. There they moved cautiously forward until a sentry stepped into Taylor's torch light, leveled his musket at them, and barked, "Identify yourself. Friend or foe?"

"We are unarmed. You can put up your rifle," said Taylor quietly. "We're here to find Lieutenant Colonel Kane of the 1st Pennsylvania Rifles."

"You mean you-all's surrenderin'?" replied the soldier in a scornful Southern drawl. "Hey, Sergeant. We got ourselves a couple of Yankees over here."

Another soldier appeared out of the brush and commanded, "You bluebellies lie on the ground an' put your arms behind your backs 'til we search you. Keep a close look out, Private, to make sure this ain't no Yankee trick."

After the sergeant roughly frisked Taylor and Jimmy, he pushed them at gunpoint through the dark woods and back to a clearing where several low fires sputtered and smoked in front of a row of sagging tents. A squad of Rebel soldiers jumped up from the nearest fire when the prisoners were escorted into camp. The Rebs crowded closer to examine the Yankees as if they were some rare specimens.

"Well, I'll be danged," said a dirty-looking private, spitting tobacco juice from his stained lips. "It's a couple o' them Bucktailed fellas we sent packin' back yonder in them woods. What's wrong, boys, you-all run the wrong way?"

"We need to speak with an officer," grunted Captain Taylor.

"Ain't we good enough for the likes of you?" drawled another Rebel. "Where's your muskets? Throwed them away so you-all could run faster?"

"That's enough," commanded a stately looking general who stepped from a nearby tent. The officer had a bald head and piercing eyes. A bushy beard spilled over his collar and partially hid the stars embroidered there.

The Rebels stepped back from the prisoners and snapped to attention. The general continued, "I am Richard Ewell, and I see that you are Pennsylvania Wildcats. Excuse my men's ill manners, gentlemen. I know how hard you fought today, and I salute you. What's your reason for coming to my camp?"

"General Ewell, sir," replied Captain Taylor. "We surrendered of our own free will to come look for our commanding officer, Lieutenant Colonel Thomas Kane, who was wounded this evening and wouldn't let us carry him to safety. When we didn't find him among the dead, we assumed he was brought here."

"You are right, Captain, but I have no idea where he's been taken. It's too dark to look for him. I'm sure he's in good hands. If you gentlemen wish to return to your regiment, I will gladly parole you."

"No, thank you, General. We've come to look after our colonel, and that's what we aim to do," replied Taylor.

"Very well. Consider yourselves my prisoners. I will send an escort with you tomorrow, so that you may find your Colonel Kane and tend to him. For now, find a place by the fire."

"Thank you, General. I also wanted to tell you that you still have wounded men out on the battlefield. I'm afraid some of them won't last the night unless they get help."

"Thank you, Captain. I'll send these malingerers to bring them back. If they have enough energy to mock brave men, they will have more than enough for this mission of mercy."

That night Captain Taylor and Jimmy slept by the fire with their Reb captors. Jimmy woke sweating several times from dreams of hands grabbing him and strangled voices begging for water. When Taylor shook Jimmy by the shoulder to wake him at dawn, the private sat up in horror, stifling a scream.

The same sergeant who brought Taylor and Jimmy into camp acted as their guide on their trip behind the Rebel lines. First, they checked unsuccessfully with several breakfasting regiments and then proceeded south on the valley turnpike until they caught up with Jackson's supply train. There they found a delirious Lieutenant Colonel Kane lying on an ammunition wagon in the boiling sun. Kane was practically naked because someone had robbed him of his bucktailed hat, officer's tunic, and black boots.

"Colonel Kane," gasped Captain Taylor. "Can you hear me?"

Kane was talking gibberish and snatching at invisible gnats he complained of in less than dignified language until the captain and Jimmy climbed into the wagon. Taylor washed the lieutenant colonel's wounds with water from his canteen and bandaged them with the lining he tore from his coat. Jimmy, meanwhile, applied a wet cloth to Kane's burning forehead. To shield Kane from the sun, Jimmy fashioned a crude umbrella from his jacket.

"Now, I see why the Lord led me here," said Jimmy, after they had made their leader more comfortable. "If we hadn't come, I don't see how the colonel would have made it."

"Oh, he'd have made it all right," assured Captain Taylor. "It'll take more than a couple of Reb bullets to stop a man with the colonel's grit."

The ammunition wagon continued on its way. Fortunately, Lieutenant Colonel Kane's fever broke after the soldiers had traveled another hour up the Shenandoah Valley. Traffic on the road was light, with only an occasional cavalry patrol passing by. This enabled the wounded officer to sleep fitfully until they reached the village of Cross Keys. There the driver was hailed by a weasely faced cavalry sergeant and pulled off the road to receive orders.

After the courier had delivered his message, he studied the Union prisoners with interest and then said sarcastically, "So, the brave Colonel Kane has finally met his match. I heared how you fellas got slaughtered by the 1st Maryland. They even put a bucktail on their flagpole ta celebrate their victory over ya."

When Jimmy returned the man's gaze and found himself face-to-face with Jeb Starr, he muttered, "It was you I saw burning the bridge over the North Fork."

"An' I enjoyed every minute of it, too."

"You know, I believed all along that you went south at Manassas to escape Sergeant Curtis' search party."

"I had to. Them boys was good trackers an' woulda caught me fer sure. I jess followed the railroad grade south 'til I met a Reb company an' threw myself at their mercy. They was real glad ta sign me up after they learned I was an almighty Bucktail scout."

"How did the likes of you get into the cavalry, let alone make sergeant?" marveled Captain Taylor. "I didn't think you knew one end of a horse from the other."

"Captain, I know which end you remind me of," sneered Starr.

"It's too bad changing coats didn't bring with it a change of heart," shot back Jimmy, "but that would be a miracle that even God couldn't perform."

"Well, I'd like ta stay an' chat with you fellas, but I gotta git orders 'round to our boys in the mountains up yonder. I hope you-all have a nice long stay here in the South—in one of our prisons."

"And, Starr, I hope you have an even longer stay in hell," said the awakening Kane.

Chapter Fourteen

BUCKY'S QUEST

While Jimmy and Captain Taylor attended to Lieutenant Colonel Kane in the ammunition wagon, Sergeant Curtis' squad dug seven graves at the edge of the Harrisonburg battlefield. A truce had been called, and the Confederates were similarly engaged a short distance away.

"It's too gol-dang hot fer this kind o' work," grumbled Curtis, wiping the sweat from his eyes with a soiled handkerchief.

"I'd say the same in December," added Boone.

"If it makes ya feel any better," said Frank, "them Rebs is diggin' ten more holes than us."

"I jess wish Jimmy would git back," muttered Bucky. "I'm worried 'bout him, an' we need him ta speak over these fellas. I swear he knows the whole Bible by heart an' kin pray easy as most folks breathe."

"If Jimmy ain't back by now," said Frank, "the Rebs got him."

"Why don't we ask them Rebs over yonder?" suggested Boone. "Maybe they know somethin'."

"Wouldn't that be con-sortin' with the enemy?" warned Sergeant Curtis.

"Con-whating?" laughed Boone. "Come on, Sergeant. Let me try."

"I don't know."

"Come on. Ya wanna find out what happened ta Captain Taylor an' Jimmy, don't ya?"

"Okay. But don't give no information back."

Boone threw down his shovel and sauntered toward the Rebel gravediggers. When he had covered half the distance to their position, he shouted, "Hey, any o' you Johnny Rebs heard 'bout a coupla Bucktails bein' captured last night? One o' our boys was a captain an' the other a private barely outta diapers."

"Well, Billy Yank. Mebbe we did, an' mebbe we didn't," drawled one of the gravediggers, leaning on a pick. "What's it worth to you-all?"

"Those fellas was friends o' ours. We was jess curious is all."

"We don't know nothin'—unless you might have some coffee you'd be willin' to part with."

Frank strode to Boone's side and said, "I have some that I might give you Rebs if ya really do know anything besides how ta dig a hole."

"Jess lay that there coffee on the ground, an' open them big Yankee ears."

After Frank produced two small bags of coffee from his coat and reluctantly tossed them in the direction of the Rebels, the gravedigger continued, "There was a coupla fellas surrendered las' night. Jess walked into camp like they owned the place an' then refused parole when it was offered. Dangest thing I even seen. Don't know nothin' else 'cept they's now our prisoners."

"How 'bout Colonel Kane?" asked Boone. "Was he in yer camp, too?"

"Can't say as I's seen no Yank colonel. That is unless you boys has salt pork or fresh biscuits you ain't plannin' to eat."

"Sorry," grinned Boone, "but the weevils ate all we had. Don't go givin' none o' that coffee ta yer drummer boys. They's already too dizzy ta keep a right proper beat."

"So Jimmy did get captured," said Bucky quietly when Boone and Frank returned.

"Hey, jess be glad we ain't diggin' a hole fer him," grunted Curtis. "Come on. Let's wrap them bodies in blankets an' git this over with. Don't matter how many burials I been to. They still gives me the creeps."

The Bucktails lowered their slain comrades into the graves and covered them carefully with dirt. Then Hosea Curtis recited the Lord's Prayer in a deep, clear voice and asked God to accept the men's souls into heaven. When he had finished, Frank wondered aloud, "Where did ya learn ta pray, Hosea? It sure weren't in no tavern."

"I guess I been hangin' 'round Jewett too much. An' jess 'cause a fella likes a little corn liquor once in awhile don't mean he ain't got religion."

"Right," joshed Boone, "an' the next thing you're gonna tell us is that *yer* pa was a preacher man."

"Never mind, Boone. Let's go," growled the sergeant. "I'll bet ya won't even take yer own funeral serious."

Curtis and his squad shouldered their shovels and retraced their steps to Harrisonburg. There they found that Dan Lemon and a half-dozen other stragglers had returned from down the valley. The men looked well rested, and they were passing out hardtack they had brought with them.

"Nice o' you fellas ta drop in now that the battle's over," grumbled Curtis.

"An' the buryin', too," added Frank.

"Sorry, but I ain't as young as the rest o' ya," apologized Dan. "I tried ta keep up with the fatigue march, but these old legs went an' failed me."

"Dan, where did you fellas rest up?" asked Bucky.

"After we got too tuckered ta go any farther, we stayed in Woodstock fer a coupla days an' marched slow an' easy down ta here."

"It looks like you fellas wasn't the only ones we wore out," chuckled Hosea. "I heared that the Flyin' Brigade ain't got enough horseshoes left ta keep goin'. Most o' their mounts is done fer anyhow. I'll bet Colonel Kane'll be pleased ta know that his tactics worked. After this campaign, nobody'll argue that we're more de-pendable scouts than a gol-dang cavalry."

"I'm sure glad we outlasted Bayard's boys," added Frank. "I got mighty tired of 'em callin' us coffee boilers an' such. Who's gonna be sittin' 'round boilin' coffee now?"

"Oh, before I forgot," interrupted Dan. "I got a letter fer ya, Sergeant Curtis."

Curtis took the badly stained envelope from Lemon and tore it open with one swipe of his bear-sized hand. "Well, I'll be dipped," he said with a grin. "It's from Joe Keener o' Company K. He wrote me from Falmouth. He's the fella that used ta work on my loggin' crew before he moved down Clearfield way back in '59. He kin stack manure even higher than Boone."

Hosea began skimming the letter until he laughed so hard he set it aside to regain his composure. Then Boone said, "What's so funny, Sergeant? If that there epistle is so dang amusin', why don't ya read it ta the rest o' us? Some o' these fellas need cheerin' up after all the dang killin', buryin', and Bucktail capturin' that's been goin' on 'round here."

"Okay, Boone, but the fellas might not consider ya the head joker no more after they hear what Keener says:

Howdy Hosea,

How's things out yonder in Shenandoah Country? We heared that Old Jack's been playing fox and geese with you fellas, but that's a far stretch fer me ta believe. But I do know Jackson's a sly old rascal and learned how ta pluck poultry outta a hen house at a young age. I heared he got the name Stonewall because that's the only thing saved him from getting shot by the farmer he robbed.

Colonel McNeil ain't recovered from the fever yet, so Major Stone's still our babysetter. The major's job's been real easy, too, because the rest of us Bucktails is jess waiting around Falmouth getting calluses on our behinds. I guess that makes us perfect fer the <u>rear guard</u>.

Rumor has it that all six companies of us will be shipped off ta the Peninsula before long. Of course, the general's idea of <u>before long</u> has a lot more <u>long</u> in it than anything.

At least I learned a new way of fishing when I wasn't fiddling er whittling here in Falmouth. I jess roll a cannon loaded with grape-shot up ta a likely pool, point its muzzle inta the water, and touch her off. Ya can't believe how successful this is. With one blast, I get enough fish ta feed the whole regiment. You've heard of shooting fish in a barrel? With a Napoleon howitzer, I kin take on the whole river.

Joe Keener

P.S. I'd have used 'Yer friend' in closing, but I'd <u>never</u> live that down."

When the sergeant had finished reading, his squad howled with laughter until their sides hurt. They begged Curtis to read the letter over and over until everyone had the jokes memorized. They capped off their fun by heckling Boone about being dethroned as the regiment wit. Finally, Boone shot back, "There's more corn in that letter than you'll find in a whole crib after the harvest. I think up better jokes in my sleep than that Keener fella writes when he's awake."

"How come we ain't heared none of 'em?" laughed Frank.

Bucky wasn't amused by the sergeant's reading. He sat staring off to the south, oblivious to the fun going on around him. After the other men wandered off to take a nap, Bucky sought out Dan Lemon and said, "I was wonderin', Dan, if you'd do me a favor?"

"What's that, Bucky?"

"I need ta have someone write Mrs. Jewett an' tell her 'bout Jimmy an' Scarecrow. You're the only other fella I know besides Jimmy who kin write worth a lick."

"Sure, Bucky. I'll be glad ta help ya. Let me fetch some paper an' a steel pen outta my haversack. There they are. First chance I got to use 'em with no wife ta write to. Okay. What do ya wanna say?"

"I been thinkin' about it some an' . . . here goes:

Dear Mrs. Jewett,

I'm a plain speakin' fella an' ain't much fer beatin' 'round the bush. Us Bucktails was in a terrible fight last evenin' near a little place called Harrisonburg. A lot o' our boys was hurt in this battle. Sam Whalen was one of 'em. He got stabbed in the side an' died o' his wound. I'm powerful sorry, ma'am. I done my best ta help him. I want ya ta know that.

Colonel Kane was also hurt real bad. He got shot in the leg an' the chest. He wouldn't let us carry 'im off an' got captured by the Rebs. I'm afraid that Jimmy got captured, too, when him and Captain Taylor went lookin' fer the colonel. Try not ta worry, ma'am, though I know it'll be hard. As far as we know, Jimmy ain't hurt er nothin'. Have Mr. Jewett pray ta yer God fer Jimmy. I know that'll help. I'll be sure ta send more news when I hear it.

Yer friend,

Bucky"

"Ain't ya even gonna tell 'em ya got promoted?" asked Dan after he finished writing. "Ya should send 'em some good news, too, ya know."

"No, I ain't real proud o' my new stripes. If I'da been able ta save Scarecrow, it might be different."

"Hey, ya can't blame yerself fer what happened. Ya didn't stab the little fella. An' if he'da had any starch, he'da defended hisself. He did have a sword, ya know."

"I can't help but feel bad."

"Are ya sure ya don't want me ta add ta yer letter?"

"No. That's all I want ta say."

"Okay, Bucky. I'll stick it in an envelope an' take it up ta headquarters fer ya. They'll send it out."

"Thanks, Dan."

Bucky turned his back on his friends and wandered off into a dark grove of hemlocks. There he stripped off his uniform and hid it in a hollow tree with his musket. He took the knife his father, Iroquois, had given him and shaved the hair from the sides of his head until only a scalp lock ran down the center of his skull. He knelt near a trickling spring, scooped up mud, and smeared it all over his body. Thus camouflaged, he slunk away to the south, armed only with his knife and his intense hatred of those who had snatched away his colonel and his best friend.

The Indian moved through the gathering dusk as swiftly as his brother the wind and as silently as a shadow. He could feel all his old instincts returning while he slipped through the Rebel rear guard like mist and spied on several regiments without spotting Jimmy or Kane. He went all the way to Cross Keys undetected. The Rebels there were heaping up stones, dirt, and logs to prepare a battle line, and Bucky stole warily around the enemy flank.

Bucky slipped through the gloom until he came to the Confederates' main camp. Outside headquarters, four bearded officers were gathered around a fire discussing strategy. Nearby, several orderlies were unloading boxes from a supply wagon into a surgery tent. To the left of the field hospital was another large tent guarded by two half-awake Rebel guards. Bucky crawled toward it when he swore he heard Lieutenant Colonel Kane's delirious voice rumble through the canvas walls. The Indian slithered along like a deadly snake to within five feet of this tent when Jimmy's voice said, "Now, Colonel, you know you're in no shape to try an escape. You can't tear open your wounds again, or you'll risk infection. Isn't that right, Captain Taylor?"

Bucky was so startled by his friend's announcement that he banged his knee on a rock that he squirmed over. When the Indian grunted in pain, the first sentry said to his partner, "Did you-all hear somethin', Bo?"

"I reckon I heard that crazy colonel plottin' his escape again," replied the second Reb.

"No, I mean somethin' outside the tent. Mebbe I'd best have me a look."

The first sentry was a brittle stick of a man, and when he came into the shadows, Bucky easily overpowered him and drove his knife between the thin soldier's ribs. The Indian slid the dead man noiselessly to the ground and crouched waiting for the other sentry to come looking for his friend. Instead, Bucky heard a familiar voice shout to the remaining guard, "Is everything all right, Private?"

"I ain't sure, Sergeant. Henry went alongside the tent there 'cause he thought he heard a noise. Henry? Is you all right?"

Bucky froze in the shadows, poised for an attack. Around the corner of the tent came a short Reb holding a torch that illuminated his vicious face. He was accompanied by a taller private armed with a rifle, held cocked and ready. Bucky had a hard time stifling his surprise when he saw that the shorter soldier was Jeb Starr.

Bucky leaped while he still had surprise in his favor and drove his knife through Starr's coat. The blade missed its mark, and the scrawny sergeant dropped his torch in the ensuing scuffle. The other sentry dared not shoot at the wrestling men for fear of hitting his comrade. He kept sidling closer to the combatants until Bucky kicked the Reb's rifle from his quivering hands. Then the Indian drove his fist into Starr's sternum, knocking the fight out of him. Before he could stab Starr, the other Reb recovered his gun, and Bucky leaped up and bolted off into the woods. The sentry fired wildly but only his muzzle flash hit the fleeing Indian.

Pandemonium followed Bucky's flight. There were shouts, more gunshots, and the hurried assembling of men. Within minutes, the Indian saw a skirmish line of torches form behind him and press forward in urgent pursuit. Bucky slipped noiselessly through the trees as the Rebs cursed and howled at his heels. They were within fifty yards of overtaking him when he shinnied up a tree trunk and froze motionless above his pursuers. Starr passed right beneath him brandishing his torch like a sword. "It was Culp. Stinkin' Culp," raged the sergeant to another soldier. "When we catch 'im, I'm gonna personally cut out his heart."

While Bucky hid in the tree, he thought about how close he'd come to rescuing his cohorts. He knew it was no use returning for a second try with the whole camp on alert. He also figured that tomorrow the prisoners would be moved. "Dang," Bucky whispered to himself, "if it weren't for that weasel, Starr, I'da freed Jimmy an' the colonel sure as shootin'."

Bucky waited until the torches were dim flickers in the distance before he climbed to the ground. There was little use attempting to escape through the dark woods with the place crawling with Rebs, so he veered off to his right, hoping to hit the valley turnpike. The moon came up, and he used its light to guide him into a meadow and onto the very road he was looking for. To hide his profile from searching enemy eyes, he ran bent at the waist and kept to the brush line bordering the turnpike. Several times he had to lie motionless in a ditch until cavalry patrols clattered past going north. One such patrol was led by Starr, who was still cursing Bucky's name as he galloped past in a whirlwind of dust.

The sun was just breaking over the horizon when Bucky returned exhausted to the grove of hemlocks where he had stashed his uniform. He fetched it from the hollow tree and was just stepping into his trousers when Boone appeared from behind another hemlock and said, "I saw ya slink off last evenin'. Where ya been?"

"I was countin' coup."

"Countin' what?"

"Coup. In the tradition of my father, Iroquois. It's a test o' bravery ta go inta an enemy's camp an' steal his most prized po-ssession."

"An' what might that be?"

"Freedom fer Jimmy, Captain Taylor, an' Colonel Kane. I'm jess sorry I failed."

"An' ya went without yer uniform?"

"Yep. Goin' naked an' covered with mud made me a lot harder ta see after dark. Coats has shiny buttons that glow in the moonlight. Boots make noise stepping on rocks an' logs. You should know that after all the huntin' ya done."

"Bucky, promise me you'll never sneak outta camp like this again. If the Rebs woulda caught ya outta uniform, they'da shot ya fer a spy. If our boys caught ya, they'd think ya was a deserter. You'd lose yer stripes an' might even git flogged."

"Okay, Boone. I promise. Besides, there ain't no use lookin' fer Jimmy now that the Rebs is all stirred up."

"Hey, an' ya better cover up that scalp lock. Sergeant Curtis'll have ya on midnight guard duty fer the rest o' yer life if he sees ya like that. Don't ya remember him tellin' us how his folks was butchered by Indians? You know how long it took him ta accept ya because o' it."

"Don't worry. I won't be seein' the sergeant today 'cause I can't do no marchin' after last night."

"What happened anyhow, Bucky?"

"I made it all the way ta Reb headquarters an' found Jimmy. I woulda freed him an' the rest, too, if it weren't fer Starr."

"Ya mean Jeb Starr?"

"Yeah, he's joined up with the Rebs, an' he led the search party that almost caught me. I'll tell ya the rest later. Now, I'm in real bad need o' some sleep. Tell the sergeant I've gone ta General Bayard's camp. I'll catch up with ya when I kin."

Bucktail officers were renowned for their fearlessness when leading their men into battle. Their bravery often brought dire consequences. Thomas Kane was severely wounded at Dranesville and Harrisonburg. Colonel Hugh McNeil was killed at Antietam during a bold charge across a plowed field.

Courtesy of Rich Adams

This older soldier tried to give himself an advantage if he were captured. Notice the symbol on his canteen, coat, and hat. It's a Masonic sign. If he surrendered to a Confederate Mason, his treatment would be better.

Chapter Fifteen

CROSS KEYS

"Seems like all we do is march an' fight, fight an' march," griped Sergeant Curtis as his squad plunged into a little wood in support of Captain Buell's battery of Pierrepont guns.

"At least we had yesterday ta rest up some," said Frank.

"That's everybody 'cept Bucky," beamed Boone. "Did I tell you fellas how he went off by hisself last night an' come within a gnat's wink of rescuin' Jimmy, Colonel Kane, an' Captain Taylor, ta boot?"

"Only 'bout thirty times," groaned Curtis.

"Well, Bucky only took on the whole Reb army singlehanded. No wonder he's too tuckered out ta join us on our little invasion o' Cross Keys."

"I still wanna hear Culp's version o' the story," growled the sergeant, "before I de-cide if he's entitled ta an extra day's rest. I'm gonna go real hard on him if what ya told me is hogwash, Boone. I wish Culp was here, myself. We need all the men we kin throw at them Rebs."

"Cross Keys sure is a queer name fer that little village down yonder," Dan Lemon remarked.

"Captain McDonald says it's named after a tavern," replied Curtis.

"Then you'll wanna be the first one ta capture it, won't ya, Sergeant?" snickered Boone.

"Instead o' crackin' jokes," barked Curtis, "I'd be watchin' my be-hind, Boone. I'm gonna do jess that 'til I find out how good a leader this here McDonald fella is. I reckon he got put in charge o' our regiment 'cause he's the highest rankin' officer left. I heared he done a good job leadin' Company G, but I always likes ta make up my own mind."

The Bucktails crouched behind trees, listening to the clatter of small arms fire from the Union infantry's attack on a wooded ridge just ahead. General Ewell's Confederates occupied this high ground, and when Buell's battery and the Bucktails were ordered forward, Rebel howitzers began lobbing shells at them. Most of the shells fell short, but one round exploded in the midst of the 1st Rifles, blowing one soldier sky-high. He fell moaning to the ground with a broken bone protruding from his right leg. Two privates hurried to carry him from the field to safety.

To escape Reb cannon fire, Captain McDonald led the way into a shallow ravine. Before Buell's battery could be wheeled into position, shells from the Union artillery began raining down on them.

"Damn," shouted Captain McDonald. "Looks like we're too far to the right."

"Yes, sir," howled Sergeant Curtis. "Now, we's caught in a gol-dang crossfire."

Hurriedly, the Pierrepont guns were hooked back up to their caissons, and Buell and the Bucktails scrambled farther to the left. They had almost reached the protection of a high bank when a Union shell exploded in their midst, knocking Lieutenant Winslow flat. Winslow lay still for a few moments, jumped back up, and ran faster than he had before.

"Look," cackled Boone, when he saw Winslow's pants had been blown half off. "The lieutenant's okay, 'cept for a mortal wound ta his trousers."

Using the high bank as a rampart, Buell's cannon finally were brought to bear, and the Bucktails sprawled on the ground well behind them to observe the show. The Pierrepont guns spewed flames, and the 1st Rifles cheered whenever a direct hit ravaged the distant Confederate lines.

"Look at them gunners scramblin' 'round like monkeys," chuckled Sergeant Curtis as he watched the crews reload their field pieces. "They's makin' me dizzy, fast as they move."

"I never figgered they could get off four shots a minute," enthused Frank. "I'm jess glad them barrels is pointed in the Reb's di-rection."

"This is the first time I kin remember watchin' a fireworks show in the middle o' a Sunday afternoon," laughed Boone.

"I wouldn't be gettin' too comfortable if I were you, Private Crossmire," warned Captain McDonald. "Listen. Do you hear that musket fire? Doesn't it seem to be getting closer?"

"It sure do, sir," replied Curtis. "An' here comes the 27th Infantry. See their flag. There must be a retreat."

"Looks like it's time to skedaddle, Sergeant. Over to that clump of woods to our left."

The commander of the 27th Pennsylvania sprinted up to Captain McDonald and began chattering madly. Buell joined the conference moments later. The Bucktails were sent scrambling for the woods, followed by the infantry and the battery. The soldiers dashed into the forest running full speed and did not slow until they reached a wooded knoll that afforded them a good view of the surrounding countryside.

The Union force no sooner had taken its position on the knoll than it found its way blocked by a Mississippi regiment that formed up at the bottom of the slope directly below them. When more Confederates could be heard moving in on both flanks, Curtis growled, "These woods is crawlin' with gol-dang Rebs. Looks like we's in the jaws of another trap."

"That may be true, Sergeant," howled Captain Buell, "but we'll hurt them Rebs badly before they take my guns."

"Curtis, enough of that kind of talk," barked Captain McDonald. "Get down, boys. We'll give them Rebs hell when they charge us."

Only two or three minutes passed before the Rebs came rushing up the slope yelling like banshees. The Bucktails and the Pennsylvania infantry fired a devastating volley. Then they fixed bayonets and rushed forward to plague the reeling enemy. Sergeant Curtis, still stinging from his captain's rebuke, drove his bayonet clear through the first Reb he encountered. Frank and Boone were equally ferocious and downed two men each before Curtis had planted his foot on the dead Reb's chest and yanked his bayonet free.

The counterattack threw the Mississippi troops back on their heels, and the Pennsylvania soldiers cut through the Rebs' ranks like a sickle through ripe wheat. Flailing with bayonets and rifle butts, they drove the Rebels backward until Captain Buell shouted, "Regroup, men. Regroup. We've got to cover our flank before we're hit from a different direction."

The Bucktails retreated to the top of the hill just as the Rebels massed for another attack. Five Reb regiments had now entered the fray, and the pinchers of their trap closed tighter by the second.

"The Rebs may think they got us," growled Frank, "but their ranks'll have some gapin' holes in 'em before these cannon is lost."

"You're gol-dang right," whooped Hosea Curtis.

Seeing a slight gap in the Rebel lines, Captain Buell unlimbered two cannon and had them loaded with grapeshot. The gunners poured a horrific fire into the Confederates until the gap widened enough to attempt an escape. Quickly, the cannon were hitched to their caissons, and the battery made a bold dash for safety with the 27th Pennsylvania and the Bucktails right behind.

When Buell's detachment cleared the Rebel lines and burst from the wood, a confused Union battery opened fire with an accurate bombardment that showered the escaping troops with fountains of earth. One shot struck a caisson, killing two horses, and another blew up within a few feet of the Pennsylvania infantry.

"What's wrong with them gol-dang fools?" bellowed Sergeant Curtis. "Do we look like stinkin' Rebs?"

"For God's sake, wave your flag," ordered Captain McDonald to the colorbearer. "Pray that they recognize our flag."

The soldier scurried from the Bucktail ranks wildly wagging the colors. His face flushed with the exertion, and he knocked off his hat in the exuberant execution of his duty.

When the shelling from the Union battery ceased, Boone howled hoarsely, "That did it, Captain. You saved our bacon, sure as shootin'."

"Yes, sir, Captain McDonald," shouted Curtis. "Ya sure do think quick on yer feet."

"Save your congratulations," grunted McDonald. "There's Reb cavalry comin'."

Again Buell's men dashed forward across the open field separating the two armies. The Rebel cavalry closed so quickly that the Union batteries dared not resume their fire without hitting Buell. The Bucktails wheeled to face the charging horsemen and unleashed a volley that blew ten shrieking troopers from their saddles. The Rebel Yell did not sound as menacing after that, and soon the cavalry veered off and fled back into the wood.

"That was awful close," sighed Dan Lemon after the 1st Rifles had followed Buell's artillery into the cheering Union lines.

"Closer than an Injun haircut," growled Hosea. "At least we learned that McDonald is one cool fella under fire. Why, he's got almost as much grit as Lieutenant Colonel Kane hisself."

"Yeah, an' thank God we was able ta git away with all seven o' our wounded," sighed Frank with relief.

"Look. Ain't that General Fremont comin'?" asked Dan, pointing to a brisk, bearded officer dressed in a gaudy uniform, complete with a bright yellow sash.

"I reckon so," laughed Boone, "'cause we's too close ta the front fer it ta be a bantam rooster."

Accompanied by Colonel Pilsen, the chief of artillery, the general approached Buell's command and gave the men an appreciative salute. While Fremont held a discussion with Buell, Pilsen mingled with the Bucktails, shaking each rifleman's hand. "I want to thank you boys personally for saving my best battery," he said with a broad grin.

"And I want to make sure you men get fed," added Fremont. "You are now free to return to my headquarters where my cook will give you food from my own table. After all, I can't have brave men such as yourselves live forever on half rations."

The Bucktails smartly saluted the gracious general and then filed off to Fremont's headquarters. They hadn't gone far before they saw units retreating from all parts of the field.

"Looks like the gol-dang Rebs'll escape now," grumbled Sergeant Curtis. "All they gotta do is cross one more bridge an' burn it behind 'em. That'll keep us from joinin' Shields, an' tomorrow Old Jack will eat that general fer breakfast."

"Speakin' o' breakfast," said Dan, smacking his lips, "I wonder what Fremont's cook will pre-pare for us."

"Nothin' if it's fer breakfast," snickered Boone. "Don't ya see it's already late afternoon? Now fer dinner he might fix us somethin', an' it'll be a sight better than the crow the Rebs wanted ta feed us."

"I think we should send someone ta find Bucky," added Frank, "so he don't miss out on the general's grub."

"You go then," ordered Hosea. "We wouldn't want Culp pickin' up no bad habits from Bayard's boys. Bein' an Injun an' all, he's got enough on his own."

"Ah, Sergeant, ya still ain't holdin' that against Bucky, are ya?" asked Boone.

"No. Culp's proved hisself after cartin' out Scarecrow like he done. After what we been through, I ain't even gonna ask him 'bout that adventure that kept him outta this battle. I had jess about enough excitement fer one day."

"I jess thought I'd check," grinned Boone, "'cause I figured you'd be in a bad mood bein' that the Rebs still hold the Cross Keys tavern."

Chapter Sixteen

PAROLE AT LAST!

To Lieutenant Colonel Kane, Jimmy, and Captain Taylor, the Battle of Cross Keys was nothing more than the distant rumble of artillery thunder. At dawn they were hustled into a wagon and were well on their way down the valley turnpike before Fremont mounted his attack. The wounded Kane was stretched out on a straw pallet and was still in considerable agony. The lieutenant colonel never complained, but Jimmy noticed him grimace whenever the wagon rattled over the bigger bumps in the road.

"Sounds like more than a skirmish going on behind us," said Captain Taylor when the wind brought them the repeated boom of cannons from Cross Keys.

"I hope our boys are giving them hell," groaned Kane.

"If Fremont wins, do you think the Union army will free us?" asked Jimmy with a hopeful expression.

"Not unless our cavalry catches up before we cross the South Fork," said Taylor, "and that's mighty unlikely."

"What was all that commotion outside our tent last night?" asked the lieutenant colonel, wincing with pain. "I don't remember too much with the dang fever attacking me again."

"It sounded like an escape attempt to me, Colonel," replied Taylor, "and whoever it was must have gotten away if the Rebs' cursing was any indication. By the way, sir, do you have any idea what happened to Captain Blanchard? Private

Jewett and I searched the battlefield for over an hour but found no trace of him."

"Yes, I saw Will being carted away by the Rebels just before they found me. He looked in pretty bad shape, but he's a tough fellow and should survive. I just hope that the scoundrels who stole my uniform and boots didn't make off with the captain's belongings as well."

"That was low of them to take advantage of you when you were badly wounded," agreed Jimmy sympathetically.

"I can always get a new coat," replied the lieutenant colonel, "but how am I going to replace the special memento that was in the pocket of my old one?"

"And what was that, sir?" asked Taylor.

"The beautiful pipe carved for me by Private Culp."

Kane continued to question his companions to fill in the gaps in his memory while the wagon jostled through rich Shenandoah farmland. Neat farmhouses sat in the middle of pillaged fields, and barns were missing the usual braying and bleating of livestock. Other fields looked trampled as if by maneuvering cavalry. While Kane surveyed the damage, he couldn't help but feel sorry for the farmers who would go hungry that winter because they had provided forage for Stonewall Jackson's army.

After several miles the wagon descended a slope toward a swift-moving river. When they approached the bridge at the bottom of this incline, the lieutenant colonel could see Rebels swarming like locusts in the village on the other side. Kane remembered that this town was called Port Republic from a map he had studied in General Bayard's tent.

"It looks like Jackson split his army," observed Captain Taylor after they clattered across the bridge and passed several regiments gathered on the street. "Otherwise, these troops would be at Cross Keys."

"He had to," whispered Kane. "General Shields is coming from Luray to smash these devils. If only Shields could have joined up with Fremont, even Old Jack wouldn't have stood a snowball's chance."

The wagon continued through the little town until it reached Rebel headquarters at the Port Republic Inn. After stopping on the shady side of the building, the driver climbed from his seat, pumped some water from a well for himself, and then offered Lieutenant Colonel Kane a cold drink.

"I reckon we'll be here a spell," said the driver when Kane's thirst was quenched. "You boys kin stretch your legs while I go inside for my orders an' a quick nip. I don't figure I have to tell ya not to wander off with General Jackson's boys all around."

Jimmy and Captain Taylor crawled stiffly to the ground, flexed their muscles, and pumped fresh water into their own canteens. While Jimmy took a long drink, he noticed a pale Rebel propped up against the side of the tavern that served as the Confederate hospital. The wounded Reb had been recently unloaded from another wagon, and he stared derisively at Jimmy's hat until the boy said, "Do I know you from somewhere, soldier?"

"No, but I know you skunks from the ball I took up Harrisonburg way. To think that my own cousin is the commander of you doetail scum."

"You mean Lieutenant Colonel Kane?" gasped Jimmy.

"One an' the same, fella. Why are you actin' so surprised? Didn't he tell ya that most of his family sided with the grand old Confederacy?"

"That's true," replied Kane from where he lay concealed by the sides of the wagon. "How are you, William?"

The wounded Reb grew paler still when he heard Kane's voice echo from the wagon bed. Finally he croaked, "Is that really you, Thomas? I thought you was supposed to be unstoppable. I heard how you got shot in the face at Dranesville an' never slowed a lick 'til you drove our boys from the field."

"I am pretty hardheaded, William, but this time your troops shot me in the leg and chest."

"Well, curse your Yankee hide, Thomas Leiper Kane. I hope you rot from them wounds an' become food for worms. I know I'm soon gonna be. I got no feelin' in neither of my legs."

Before the wounded man could say more, two orderlies loaded him onto a stretcher and began carting him into the hospital. "Shame on you," scolded one of the orderlies. "Is that any way to speak to a brave officer?"

"It's a good thing you're taking him away," said a flushing Taylor to the Rebel soldiers. "Wounded or not, I wasn't going to let him insult the lieutenant colonel very much longer."

Kane and his companions remained in Port Republic for the rest of the day. When the evening began to dim, they saw a cloud of dust rise above the road from Cross Keys. Soon the road was streaming with Rebel soldiers, who marched with the urgency of retreating men. An hour passed and still they came like a swarm of unwanted insects. The rear guard did not arrive until it was fully dark. They announced their presence by torching the bridge over the Shenandoah River.

The next morning the prisoners were awakened by the sound of gunfire just north of Port Republic. Lieutenant Colonel Kane muttered, "Looks like Shields is here. He's in the middle of a real hornet's nest now that Ewell's army has rejoined Jackson's."

The firing intensified for the next hour before subsiding like a passing thunderstorm. When celebrating Confederates came spilling into town, a Rebel major appeared from headquarters and approached Kane. "Sir, it appears that our boys have driven back the Federal army," said the major matter-of-factly. "I'm here to offer parole for you and your men. Do you accept, sir?"

"I'm sorry, Major, but I must refuse. I do not consider parole an honorable option."

After Captain Taylor and Jimmy also refused, the men were ordered to rejoin Kane in the wagon, and they were driven through Brown's Gap and into central Virginia. When they passed through Charlottesville, the lieutenant colonel asked, "Isn't that a funeral bell I hear tolling?"

"Yes, sir," replied Taylor, "and the sound of muskets, as well. Must be a soldier being laid to rest. I'll ask the first townsfolk we pass."

From several weeping ladies dressed in black, the prisoners learned that it was General Turner Ashby who had been buried. "Ah, poor Ashby," sighed Kane when he heard the news. "A finer gentleman I've yet to meet."

"Nor a more hated foe by our Bucktails, sir."

"How can you say that, Captain Taylor?"

"Because he is the man who shot you in the leg, sir, after you spared his life."

For the rest of the trip, the captives were loaded onto a hospital train, which had a long stopover at the University of Virginia. Here a young gentleman ambled through their car passing out provisions to wounded Confederate soldiers. When the young man tried to serve Lieutenant Colonel Kane and his companions, Kane said, "We're Union prisoners."

"This food is my father's," replied the gentleman courteously. "He meant it for brave men. I'm sure you must be one, sir."

"What is your name?" asked the lieutenant colonel.

"James Winston, sir."

"Well, James Winston, I am Thomas Kane. Your father is one of my oldest family friends."

As the hospital train continued into North Carolina, Kane's wounds mended sufficiently for him to move about the car. The bullets had never been extracted, and, at first, he limped along gingerly until he mastered the use of crutches. Captain Taylor, however, had developed a hacky cough and had become emaciated due to the meager rations that had been doled out to the prisoners.

When the train reached Salisbury, a Confederate colonel tramped aboard, accompanied by five guards. The Reb squad searched among the wounded until they found Lieutenant Colonel Kane and Jimmy sitting next to Captain Taylor's sickbed. The captain's cough had worsened, and he was burning up with fever.

"Colonel Kane, I'm here to offer you and your men parole," said the Confederate officer, clearing his throat. "I also must warn you, sir, that this train has nearly reached the end of the line for you gentlemen. The next stop is a Southern prison. This will be your last opportunity to be exchanged."

Kane felt Taylor's burning forehead and considered the pleading in Jimmy's eyes. Finally, the lieutenant colonel sighed, "I think it's time we swallow our pride and return to our regiment."

"Amen to that, sir!" exclaimed Jimmy.

"Sir, that goes for me, too," mumbled Captain Taylor. "But after all the kindness we've received here, it's soon going to be hard for me to think of these Southerners as our enemies."

The Rebel squad helped Taylor to his feet and then escorted the prisoners into Salisbury station to await a northbound train. When the prisoners had been made comfortable, the Rebel colonel said, "Good luck to you, gentlemen. From here you will proceed to the Yankees' Fortress Monroe to be exchanged for two of our officers."

"How about me?" asked Jimmy in a worried voice.

"We'll probably get back a brigadier general in trade for you," replied the Reb, winking at Kane.

Chapter Seventeen

The Night Fight

Sergeant Curtis' squad baked in the withering August heat at Brandy's Station, waiting with a work gang of other soldiers to unload a long freight train that pulled in from Fortress Monroe. Hissing steam, the engine braked to a stop, and one of the boxcar doors grated open and belched forth a boisterous group of exchanged prisoners.

Bucky was standing opposite the car when he saw Jimmy helping a haggard-looking Captain Taylor onto the station platform. Before Bucky could shout to his friend, Lieutenant Colonel Kane hobbled off the train on a pair of crutches, and the whole station exploded with cheers and shots fired in the air by sentries. The shots precipitated a stampede of soldiers rushing to welcome their wounded leader.

Kane took a couple of halting steps but then threw aside his crutches with disdain. Afterward, he bellowed, "Listen up, Bucktails. I might not be able to walk as well as you yet, but I can still ride a horse with the best of them. Now that I'm back, men, you better be ready to fight. From now on I expect each of you to carry at all times one hundred rounds of ball cartridges, forty rounds in the cartridge box, the remainder in the haversack. After being cooped up for so long, I plan to give those Rebels hell. You men, drive that ambulance wagon over here for Captain Taylor. That's all. It's good to be back, Bucktails."

When the work gang cheered itself out and filed away to unload the train, Bucky yelled, "Jimmy Jewett. Jimmy. Jimmy."

Jimmy helped Captain Taylor into the ambulance wagon before turning at the sound of his friend's voice. Then he rushed to embrace Bucky, who returned his hug in a rare, heartfelt display of emotion.

"I was so afraid I'd never see ya again," choked Bucky. "So afraid . . . I even took off my uniform an' went lookin' fer ya Indian-style."

"So that was you at Cross Keys. We thought an escaped prisoner caused all the commotion that night in the Rebs' camp. Bucky, you shouldn't have taken such a risk."

"I had ta try somethin' ta save my best friend."

"Thank you so much for trying, Bucky. You can't believe what we've been through. The lieutenant colonel and the captain were both sick, and we were going to be put in a prison camp if we didn't accept parole. What a relief it is to be free."

"I'm jess so glad you're back."

"Why, Bucky. I see you're wearing your corporal's stripes," said Jimmy, noticing the two yellow chevrons sewn on his friend's sleeve. "I'll bet you're real proud of your promotion."

"These here stripes ain't a big deal, Jimmy, compared ta gettin' captured by the Rebs. Well, I best help unload this here train before Sergeant Curtis starts yellin'."

"You know," laughed Jimmy, "I almost missed the sergeant gol-danging everything. Almost. I'll see you back at camp!"

Bucky returned to the work party just as Curtis, Boone, and Frank came up the platform toward him. "Hey, Bucky," shouted Boone. "The sergeant got another letter from his loony friend, Joe Keener. I'm really startin' ta hate that guy after what he said 'bout me at the end. An' talk 'bout corny. I don't know how these other fellas kin laugh at the stuff he tries ta pass off as jokes."

"Come on, Boone," needled Frank. "You're only makin' such a fuss 'cause you're jealous. Keener is the funniest fella I come across in all my born days."

"Next, you're gonna tell me I'm jealous o' yer mediocre shootin', too, ain't ya, Frank?"

"Knock it off, you two," growled Curtis. "Let me read this here letter ta Bucky, an' let 'im make up his own mind if it's a knee-slapper, er not."

"Go ahead, Sergeant," said Bucky. "If it's got Boone's feathers all ruffled, I gotta hear it."

"Okay, here goes. An', Boone, git yer fingers outta yer ears:

Dear Hosea,

I heared Old Jack took you fellas ta the woodshed and whipped yer behinds good fer ya out there in the Shenandoah. Well, there's more than a few sore rears here in the Peninsula, too. Only us boys got whopped by that old schoolmaster, Robert E. Lee.

Down here we got ourselves in one hellacious tussle after another. At Beaver Dam Creek we damn near got captured, and at Gaines' Mill a whole division of Rebs was looking ta grind us inta meal. Let me tell ya, we paid them back in their own coin. I fired until my gun got so hot, I scalded two charging Rebs ta death with it. When I run outta bullets, the air got so thick with my cussing, the Confederate attack couldn't break through. We got clean away while they waited fer the wind ta thin out the air some.

Well, Hosea, I'll let ya git back ta licking yer wounds. I hear a plan's in the works ta reunite us Bucktails. Them generals better hurry, er all they'll be getting from our regiment will be one good company. We gotta learn not ta fight so hard, er we'll become scarcer than hair on General Burnside's noggin.

Joe Keener

P.S. Tell that Boone fella ta hand in his jester's cap because he's met his match."

"I can't say as I blame Boone fer not likin' that little jab at the end," said Bucky after Curtis had finished reading. "He's right proud o' his jokester ways."

"Well, if I ever meet up with that fella Keener," promised Boone, "he'll soon learn where the bear hid in the buckwheat."

When Bucky completed his work duty, he returned to the Bucktails' campsite and found Jimmy gulping down a heaping plateful of pork stew and hardtack. "I never thought I'd say this in a million years," said Jimmy, "but do these rations taste good."

To Bucky, his friend looked ten pounds thinner than he'd ever seen him. Gone was the last of Jimmy's boyish plumpness, which now was replaced by muscle of the stringiest sort. His cheeks, too, were shrunken, and his broad nose, topped by spectacles, had become his dominant feature.

"Here, have some more," said Bucky, filling Jimmy's plate from a pot that hung over the campfire. "How'd them Rebs treat ya, anyhow?"

"Even though they didn't feed us much, they were very courteous. I think a lot of that had to do with Lieutenant Colonel Kane, more than anything. There's something about his bearing that commands respect."

"How 'bout Captain Taylor? He looked real bad when ya helped 'im from the train."

"I think the captain was pretty worn out before our capture, but it wasn't until we ran short of food that he got sick. I have to admire the way he walked right into that Reb camp and demanded to see Lieutenant Colonel Kane. That took a lot of courage, which no doubt will get Captain Taylor through whatever is ailing him now. What have you been up to, Bucky, the two months I was gone?"

"I don't know if ya heared, but we got whipped bad at Cross Keys an' Old Jack escaped."

"I know alright, Bucky. I was there."

"What do ya mean ya was there?"

"Well, we were being held prisoner at Port Republic when Jackson beat General Shields and made his getaway. How did you boys get to Brandy Station?"

"After losin' at Cross Keys, we marched ta a little burg called Luray an' hightailed it over the Blue Ridge Mountains ta here. That Blue Ridge country was teemin' with game, an' it was tough not ta jess quit the army an' go off huntin'. I shaved my hair into a scalp lock when I went lookin' fer ya, so it woulda been real easy ta return ta my old ways. If I'da knowed all we was gonna do in these parts was guard McDowell and Pope's headquarters, I'da been long gone."

"You really don't mean that, do you Bucky? I don't believe that you'd ever do anything that wasn't honorable."

"That's powerful nice o' ya ta say, Jimmy. By the way, I had Dan Lemon write a letter ta yer ma an' tell her 'bout you an' Scarecrow."

"How did she take the news?"

Bucky reached inside his shirt pocket and produced a tattered envelope. Handing it to Jimmy, he said, "Here. See fer yerself."

When Jimmy opened the oft-folded letter, Bucky asked, "Would ya please read it aloud, so I kin hear it, too? Ya gotta learn me ta read one of these days. I git tired o' relyin' on other men's eyes."

"I'd be glad to teach you, Bucky. Why don't you look over my shoulder, and I'll point out some of the words as we go along:

Dear Bucky,

It was so good of you to write. I was worried sick when I hadn't heard from Jimmy for so long.

It was not like him to stop sending us news. The last letter we got was from a place called Front Royal. That must have been before that Shenandoah business got started.

Sam's mother took it very hard when I told her of her son's passing. The poor woman has not eaten or slept much since. We pray for her daily and hope that the good Lord will bring her peace.

We also pray for Jimmy often. I don't see how the Lord can ignore such heartfelt prayers. I know in my very soul that Jimmy will come back to me when this terrible war has ended.

No matter what happens, Bucky, remember that you are always welcome in our home. Please write again and let us know how you're doing. May God bless and keep you.

> Love,
> Mrs. Jewett

P.S. I've been putting the money you sent me in the town bank. You will have a very tidy sum by the end of the war. Bucky, you are so smart not to waste your money like I've heard many of our boys do.

Tears flowed down Jimmy's cheek when he handed Bucky back his letter. "I'd better write Mother today," he choked. "Before she worries herself to death."

"I'm afraid yer letter writin's gonna have ta wait," barked Sergeant Curtis, hurrying into camp with Frank and Boone racing along behind him. "We've been ordered ta accompany General Pope's staff train ta Catlett's Station. When we git there, we'll be guardin' Pope's personal baggage train, too. We'd best be alert 'cause them wagons contain money chests, valuable papers, an' the general's highfalutin' gear."

Bucky and his friends scrambled to take down their tents and pack up their belongings. In less than an hour they were in marching formation, waiting for a mounted Lieutenant Colonel Kane to order them forward. When the staff wagon train lurched ahead, the drummers began their familiar cadence, and off the Bucktails tramped alongside the Orange and Alexandria Railroad to the northeast.

Bucky and Jimmy marched side-by-side, and Jimmy said after they'd gone a mile or so, "That drum cadence just doesn't sound the same without Sam up there playing. I feel so bad about losing him. He was like the little brother I never had."

"An' he had come so far," added Bucky. "When Sam first joined our company, he couldn't hardly hold a drumstick er march proper. An' look how he kept up with us durin' the fatigue march after lots o' stronger fellas fell outta line. If he coulda jess got through his first battle, I know he woulda licked his fear o' the Rebs."

"I guess I'll always remember Sam every time I hear the marching beat," sighed Jimmy. "But maybe now I'd better think about how happy I am to be out in the open country again."

"Yeah," teased Bucky, "an' you're lucky ta have a short walk on yer first day back—only fifteen miles. See how that fella Kane thanks ya fer lookin' after him like ya done."

"Well, at least in this part of Virginia it isn't mountainous like at home. I know I'll be tired and have a couple of blisters by the end of the day, but I'm still very thankful the Lord has delivered me from the hands of the Rebels. You have no idea how good it is to be back with my brothers, the Bucktails."

Bucky and Jimmy marched with their regiment well into the evening, shepherding Pope's staff wagons to Catlett's Station. There they found McDowell's staff train parked in an open field with a half-asleep regiment guarding it.

"It sure seems strange that McDowell would leave his wagons in such an unsafe place," Jimmy observed as they passed by the field.

"The general must figger they'll be okay with the whole Union army between here an' Robert E. Lee's boys," replied

Bucky. "Lately, us Bucktails know all 'bout borin' rear guard de-tails."

The Bucktails led Pope's wagon train into the shelter of a grove of trees next to Pope's personal baggage train and then set up their own camp in a field nearby. They had just erected their tents when a terrific thunderstorm sent them scurrying for cover. Bucky heard Colonel Kane order Lieutenant Winslow and fifteen others to take picket duty, and he was glad he wasn't included.

Bucky and Jimmy shared a tent with Boone, and they lay dozing on their backs listening to the rain pummel the canvas. They had barely gotten comfortable, however, when a bang other than thunder had them propped up on their elbows listening with trained ears for the unmistakable sound of gunfire.

"Did you hear that?" asked Jimmy, now wide awake. "Who in his right mind would be out shooting in such a downpour?"

"The only one I kin think o' is the sergeant's friend, Joe Keener," joked Boone, "but hopefully he's still down on the Peninsula."

Before Bucky could speculate about the gunfire, the camp reverberated with the pounding of hooves and the hair-raising screech of the Rebel Yell. The horses rushed so close to their tent entrance that Bucky slit open the back tent wall with his knife, and he and his friends bolted off into complete darkness. Using an occasional lightning flash to guide them, they fumbled their way into a distant wood where they found Lieutenant Colonel Kane assembling a group of skirmishers. Among them were Frank, Dan Lemon, and Hosea Curtis.

"What's goin' on, Sergeant?" asked Bucky when he had splashed to Curtis' side. "If it's an attack, why didn't Lieutenant Winslow sound the alarm?"

"All I know is that it's darker than the inside of a sow's belly, an' there's Rebs out there," growled Curtis. "Jess sit tight. The colonel will be tellin' us in a minute what ta do."

After sixty-eight Bucktails had straggled into the wood, Kane shouted above the thunder, "Follow me, men. Jeb Stuart's cavalry has overrun the camp. It's my guess that they're after the Cedar Run railroad bridge. They outnumber us, but we have surprise in our favor. Let's go and drive off those stinking Rebs. Forward, Bucktails."

The lieutenant colonel led his drenched soldiers up the railroad tracks toward Cedar Run bridge. While they passed the darkened Catlett train station, muzzle blasts flashed from the darkness, sending the Bucktails diving on their bellies. When an answering volley drove off the invisible enemy, Frank wondered, "What are we shootin' at? Hants?"

"They call that Reb John Mosby 'the Gray Ghost,' but I doubt if he's here," cracked Boone.

"Be careful where you're firin' yer gol-dang rifles," warned Hosea. "It's too dark ta be shootin' wild like that."

The rain continued to buffet the Bucktails as they worked their way down the tracks. When they reached the bridge minutes later, they found it deserted except for a pile of discarded torches and axes that Jimmy tripped over in the dark.

"Them Rebs musta give up the idea o' burnin' this here bridge," chuckled Boone while helping Jimmy to his feet. "In this downpour, they might jess as well have tried settin' fire ta the creek."

"The axes wouldn't do much ta that double trestle work neither," said Sergeant Curtis. "That is if they could even see it."

"I wouldn't wanna be hackin' away in the dark," added Dan. "It'd be my luck ta cut my leg clean off."

Lieutenant Colonel Kane sent out several scouts to track the movement of the enemy and to find the other hundred missing Bucktails. One of the men promptly returned to notify Kane that a large group of Reb cavalry was coming up the Manassas road. "Okay, men," ordered Kane when he heard the report, "quietly now. Let's get ourselves over there and see what damage we can do."

The Bucktails followed the scout through the gloom, and then Kane formed up his troops behind some trees along the Manassas road. When the lieutenant colonel heard the clatter of cavalry drawing near, he warned in a harsh whisper, "Wait until they're too close to miss. Then give 'em hell."

Bucky waited until the Rebels were only a few yards away before firing his rifle into the face of the enemy. Immediately, a volley rumbled from his mates' guns, blowing Rebs from their saddles and spooking their mounts. The horses shrieked and reared in the air, knocking yet more enemy cavalry to the ground. Finally, the animals stampeded, carrying what was left of the troopers away before Bucky could reload his weapon in the pitch blackness.

"That'll teach 'em ta invade our camp," howled Curtis in Bucky's ear. "Jeb Stuart be damned."

The horses thundered off into the darkness with their riders screaming curses as they tried to control their crazed mounts. Unfortunately, the stampede carried the Rebels right into the midst of General Pope's staff train. It wasn't long before Bucky could see blazing tents and wagons in the distance when the Rebs fell to plundering the camp the Bucktails should have been protecting.

"Come on, Bucktails," shouted Kane when he saw the flames. "Now, we'll have some real light to shoot by."

Following the incensed Kane, Bucky and his squad rushed forward into Pope's camp. Hiding behind trees, they picked off plundering Rebels illuminated by their own torches and by burning wagons. Confusion was everywhere. Rifles blazed. Men howled. Mules brayed. Thunder rolled. Horses shrieked. Lightning glared. Troops fell and rose no more.

At the height of the pandemonium, Lieutenant Colonel Kane leaped forward to slash at a passing cavalryman with his sword. Kane cut the man down with a vicious blow, but before he could jump back into the shadows, a Reb cavalry sergeant bore down on him from behind. "I got ya now, Colonel," howled the trooper, leveling his horse pistol at Kane. "An' I'm gonna enjoy watchin' ya die."

Before the cavalryman could discharge his pistol, Bucky popped from behind a blazing wagon and shot the Rebel squarely in the chest. The man threw his arms in the air and tumbled to the ground at Bucky's feet. Bucky rolled the body over and found himself staring at a very dead Jeb Starr, his face frozen in an eternal expression of hate. The Indian lad's eyes widened when he saw a familiar object lying next to Starr's corpse, and he picked it up and put it in his pocket.

"That fixed the traitor," growled Kane above the confusion. "Come on, Culp. Follow me."

Kane rallied his Bucktails and charged across an open field toward a mass of Stuart's cavalry. Screaming like lunatics, Bucky and his mates threw themselves at the surprised troopers. Wielding their muskets like clubs, they smashed horsemen to the ground and fought with such fury that it threw the superior Rebel force into a panic. Instead of regrouping for a counterattack, the cavalry milled in confused circles while the Bucktails continued to club, slash, and shoot at them. Finally, Stuart's men had enough and galloped in full retreat back into the wood from which they had swooped.

"Just as it says in Leviticus 26:8," shouted Jimmy when the Rebs were in full retreat, "'Five of you shall chase a hundred, and a hundred of you shall put ten thousand to flight: and your enemies shall fall before you by the sword'."

"An' by the bullet an' the rifle butt, too!" shrieked Frank.

After helping to extinguish Pope's burning staff train, Bucky and his squad returned to their camp and rolled exhausted into their blankets. They slept like dead men until the next morning when they rose to build a roaring bonfire. They huddled around it to dry out their uniforms and swap stories.

"Boy, I ain't never seen such a battle as that," said Dan, swilling a cup of hot coffee.

"Me neither," agreed Hosea Curtis. "Half the time I was afraid ta shoot, not knowin' who was a friend an' who was a gol-dang Reb."

"All that really matters is that we drove them off," said Jimmy with a relieved grin.

"Jimmy, no wonder they fled like they done," chuckled Boone. "The way you was yellin', them Rebs musta thought all hell had broke loose."

"Hey, Jimmy wasn't the only wildcat out there," said Frank. "I seen Bucky kill some fella gunnin' fer Colonel Kane."

"That wasn't jess any fella," added Dan. "That was Jeb Starr. I'd recognize him anywhere. Even hell."

"Well, I'll be dipped," growled Curtis. "It's 'bout time that gol-dang weasel met his Maker. Good shootin', Bucky."

"I wouldn't be congratulatin' him if I was you, Sergeant," chuckled Boone. "Bucky keeps savin' colonels like that, an' you'll be sayin' 'Yes, sir' ta him."

"Knock it off, Boone," muttered Bucky, reddening. "I jess done what any o' you fellas woulda. An' look what fell outta Starr's pocket when he hit the ground."

"Why, it's the pipe you carved for Colonel Kane!" exclaimed Jimmy. "So Starr was the one who stole the colonel's clothes after he was wounded and left him lying half naked in an ammunition wagon."

"After all the dirty tricks Starr pulled, why does that surprise ya?" asked Frank.

"All I know for sure," replied Jimmy, "is that Bucky better get that pipe back to Colonel Kane."

"How come?"

"Well, Bucky, because Kane considers the pipe one of his most prized possessions. I heard him say so himself."

"That's real nice an' everythin'," grunted Dan, "but I'd rather hear 'bout what old Jeb Stuart's boys made off with. Does anybody know?"

"Down at headquarters," answered Hosea, "they said the rascal took 300 prisoners, $35,000 cash money, an' General Pope's dress uniform."

"Luckily, the general wasn't in camp when the Rebs attacked, er he'd have been captured in his uniform," said Frank wryly.

"Yeah, I heared Pope likes ta boast that his headquarters are in the saddle," smirked Boone. "If ya ask me, he's got his headquarters where his hindquarters outta be."

"I just wish that Lieutenant Winslow and the other pickets had escaped capture, too," sighed Jimmy. "I sure don't envy those fellows."

"My only question is, what did Stuart want with Pope's uniform?" snickered Boone. "I doubt if old Jeb'll be attendin' any Washington balls real soon."

"I heared that Stuart was seekin' revenge fer the loss o' his favorite plumed hat stoled by some Yankee troopers," said Dan seriously.

"That sounds like a dandy reason ta attack our camp in the middle o' a de-luge ta me," cracked Boone. "But then again, I honestly enjoy gettin' soaked ta the skin an' shot at by fellas I can't even see."

"I have one other question," said Jimmy. "If the Rebs couldn't set fire to the railroad bridge in that downpour, how could they burn the wagons?"

"It ain't wet *inside* a covered wagon," smirked Frank. "Jimmy, fer a smart fella, sometimes I wonder 'bout you."

"And I wonder how the lieutenant colonel got around like he did during the battle. Why, he could barely walk when he got off the train yesterday. After the shooting started, I didn't see him limp at all," observed Jimmy in an awed voice.

"Kane was like a fella trapped in a burnin' buildin'," winked Boone. "He's gonna do his best ta git outta that situation even if his pants is hangin' in the closet."

Chapter Eighteen

STANDING FAST

"Seems like us Bucktails has been part of the rear guard forever," sighed Bucky while he and Jimmy strolled about the Federals' Bull Run Camp to pass the time.

"Yeah," replied Jimmy, "but as long as we're under Colonel Kane's command, I doubt if we'll have to worry about seeing action. Look at what happened at Catlett's Station."

"Maybe you're right, but it jess seems odd not ta be fightin' after all them battles in the Shenandoah."

"I know," mused Jimmy. "War sure is strange. Marching. Waiting. Fighting. Dying."

The sun was just peeking over the horizon when the young soldiers returned to their campsite to start their breakfast fire. The rest of the squad wasn't up yet, so Bucky and Jimmy delayed cooking and sat listening to the daybreak chorus of songbirds.

The soldiers continued to laze about until the calm of the August dawn was broken when a wagon full of soldiers rattled up the Manassas road, towing behind it a half-inflated observation balloon. The wagon dragged the balloon to the top of a little hill, and Jimmy and Bucky ran along behind like cats following a milk cart.

While the two Bucktails stared in awe, a pair of horse-drawn hydrogen generators came rushing up the hill. A dapper-looking gentleman in civilian dress jumped from the first generator while it was still stopping and began barking orders in the rapid-fire style of a seven-shot Spencer carbine. Immediately, the squad of soldiers leaped from the wagon as if it were about to explode and scrambled to pull the balloon to the ground and hook up hoses from the generators into it. Once the machines began humming, the balloon puffed out like magic to the wonder of Bucky and Jimmy.

As the soldiers rushed to attach the basket beneath the fully inflated balloon, Jimmy approached the civilian gentleman and stammered, "How far up in the air d-d-d-do you plan to go, sir?"

"Don't call me 'sir'," barked the man testily. "I'm no major general. My name is Thaddeus Lowe. You can call me 'Professor' like everybody else does."

"Well, Professor?"

"Yes. Yes, I know," interrupted Lowe. "How far in the air shall I ascend? The answer is quite simple, young fellow. I could easily rise to fifteen hundred feet for a view in excess of fifty miles. But I only need to see fifteen miles. That means I'll be going up to three hundred feet, or eighteen rods to you. I'd like to invite you along, but unfortunately the basket only holds one passenger."

"Whatcha out here so early in the mornin' fer?" asked Bucky shyly.

"General Pope, that bombastic pinch of owl dung, roused me out of my warm bed and ordered me to see if I could locate Stonewall Jackson for him. Old Jack was up to his usual tricks yesterday, if you hadn't heard. He looted Pope's supply depot at Manassas and burned everything his soldiers didn't carry away."

"So that was all the smoke we saw on the horizon last night!" exclaimed Jimmy. "Why, we wondered—"

"To further answer the other fellow's question," interjected the Professor, "morning is the best time for reconnaissance because the enemy's breakfast fires are readily visible and provide an accurate estimate of his manpower. What I'm afraid of is that Old Jack's troops are still too stuffed from yesterday's raid to need any breakfast."

Before Jimmy or Bucky could say more, the Professor instructed the soldiers to grab hold of the guide ropes used to keep the balloon from blowing away. Then Lowe climbed into the basket and dropped out bags of sand until the balloon began to ascend above the trees. His ground crew, meanwhile, fed out enough rope to allow the balloon to reach the elevation needed for reconnaissance of the surrounding countryside.

When Lowe reached the top of his ascent, he surveyed the horizon with a spy glass and began sending messages from above on a special telegraph. Bucky and Jimmy crowded closer to the wagon where the ground operator was sitting to see if they could learn what Lowe had seen. "It looks like Old Jack done disappeared," grumbled the operator after the telegraph quit rattling. "McNeil's Bucktail scouts wasn't able to find Jackson, an' I guess the Professor ain't either. Pope's gonna have a conniption fit."

Bucky and Jimmy thanked the operator, waved goodbye to the ground crew, and hurried off to camp to tell their squad what they had seen. When they arrived back at their campfire, Boone, Frank, Dan, and Curtis had just crawled out of their tents and stood yawning in the morning sun.

"I could git pretty used ta this lazy life," said Frank, stretching his arms above his head.

"I thought you'd already mastered it," ribbed Boone, "after I carried yer sorry be-hind the length o' the Shenandoah Valley."

"Hey, I walked ten times faster than you, Boone. Yer tongue was hangin' on the ground like an old dog's be-fore I broke a sweat. Bayard's boys had ta keep tellin' me ta slow down 'cause I was wearin' out their horses. An' when I was busy shootin' Rebs in the Harrisonburg woods, ya laid down an' took a nap right in the middle o' the battle."

"What do ya mean, Frank? You sayin' I'm an idler?"

"Will you fellas knock it off," ordered Sergeant Curtis. "I'm gettin' powerful tired o' yer gol-dang grousin'."

"Good morning, boys," laughed Jimmy. "I can see things haven't changed any around here. I can't wait to tell you what Bucky and I just learned."

"Go ahead," grumbled Dan. "How ya can be cheerful at this time o' day, Jimmy, is beyond me."

"Don't ya see that balloon hoverin' above the hill?" asked Bucky. "We talked ta the fella that rides it. He told us that Old Jack's on the loose again, but he couldn't spot 'im from his balloon."

"Yeah, and McNeil's not far from here either with the rest of our Bucktails," added Jimmy. "They've also been out scouting for Stonewall Jackson. It can't be long now before we become one regiment again."

"If there's gonna be another fight here at Bull Run," growled Curtis, "I hope our army makes a better showin' than the last time."

"I'd jess be satisfied if we got ta participate," added Frank. "Anything'd be better than hangin' 'round guardin' generals' tents an' wagons."

"Hey, did you boys hear how the Rebs scrounged up enough silk ta build their own balloon once they seen how useful airships was to our spies?"

"No, but I'm sure you're gonna tell us, Boone."

"'Course I am, Frank. How else is ignorant fellas like you gonna get educated?"

"Well, git on with it," ordered Sergeant Curtis.

"It seems that them Rebs was too poor ta buy enough silk, so they went out an' requisitioned dresses from every plantation belle in Virginy 'til they could build theirselves a patchwork airship o' a whole mess o' different colors."

"I'll bet they had ta get a sissy ta go up in a balloon made outta dresses," chortled Dan.

"Or maybe one of them belles volunteered," Bucky suggested.

"No, the way I heared it, General Longstreet hisself went up fer a look-see," corrected Boone. "An' them Rebels used the balloon all durin' the Seven Days' campaign 'til our boys captured it from a Reb steamer that run aground on the James River."

"Yeah, right, Boone. An' next you're gonna tell us ya personally helped all them belles outta their dresses," guffawed Frank.

For the next two days Bucky and his squad heard the distant thunder of a furious battle, but they continued to languish in camp. On the second day a fuming Lieutenant Colonel Kane assembled them into battle formation, but no word came for their call-up. Finally, a terrible barrage shook the flank of the Union lines, and a stream of fleeing blue coats came rushing from the front. Immediately, Kane ordered his men forward to the bridge over Cub Run and formed them into a battle line. Then Kane howled, "Fix bayonets, Bucktails, and stand fast. Show by your example that there's nothin' to fear from those Rebs."

Although Sergeant Curtis and his squad shouted at the retreating troops and threatened them with bayonets, the tide of fleeing men was just too strong. One frantic soldier used his head like a battering ram and drove through the Bucktail line screaming, "Longstreet's a comin'. Longstreet's a comin'. Run before we's all butchered." Even when Frank laid the coward out with a vicious blow of his rifle butt, it did little to check the panic of the soldiers bowling along at his heels.

Finally, Kane saw that his force was inadequate to quell the rout of the Union army, so he gathered his Bucktails and pressed forward toward the Rebel lines. On the way, they encountered a lieutenant commanding four mountain howitzers, and Kane badgered the artillery officer into returning to the front.

Bucky and his mates loped along beside the caissons until they reached Bull Run Bridge where three other cannons were engaging the enemy. There they helped the artillery lieutenant's depleted unit wheel the howitzers into position. Then the Bucktails formed an unbudging battle line on both sides of the bridge and stood with grim faces full of defiance. Noting the 1st Rifles' steadfast demeanor, the passing troops began to slow until the retreat once more became orderly. Bucky grinned to himself when he overheard one passing infantryman say, "Those fellas have more brass than Lincoln's whole dang passel of generals."

Night closed in rapidly, and Bucky kept expecting an enemy charge that never came. "Where are those dang Rebs?" Bucky said to Jimmy, as he watched the last of the retreating Union troops stream by. "I can't believe they ain't gonna try an' capture more o' Pope's boys."

"I can," replied Jimmy. "Lee can't even feed his own men, let alone a bunch of prisoners. I can testify to that, let me tell you."

Well past midnight Bucky heard the pounding of a horse's hooves behind him, and a courier galloped from the darkness and rushed past the pickets before he could be challenged. The cavalryman reined his horse to a stop near Lieutenant Colonel Kane, and after giving a hurried salute, said, "Sir, I'm here to offer you General Pope's congratulations for your part in the retreat. Now that our men have all safely crossed Bull Run, you are hereby ordered to destroy this bridge."

Kane saluted briskly and barked to Curtis, "You heard the man, Sergeant. Get some torches lit and get cracking. I want that bridge so engulfed in flame that even Jeb Stuart's hellhounds can't cross it."

Bucktail reenactors assemble into parade formation.

Josie Copello, wife of the captain of Company K, 1st Pennsylvania Rifles, proudly displays a bucktail in her hat. The keen observer will note the Sharps rifle hanging on the stacked muskets. Breech-loading Sharps were issued to the Bucktails after the Second Battle of Bull Run.

Chapter Nineteen

PUT-DOWNS AND PROMOTIONS

The day after the Battle of Bull Run, Lieutenant Colonel Kane's command sloshed to Alexandria in a driving rainstorm. It was too wet for the drummers to mark the cadence, so most of the march was accomplished in silence. Even the usually talkative Boone had little to say until Frank asked, "What ails ya today, fella? Yer mouth usually runs faster than a whippoorwill's be-hind in huckleberry season."

"I guess I'm jess tuckered out from guardin' Bull Run Bridge half the dang night. I'm not much fer stayin' up late, Frank. I believe days is meant fer fightin' an' nights fer sleepin'."

"Don't let Boone fool ya," chuckled Sergeant Curtis. "The only reason he ain't talkin' is 'cause he's busy thinkin' o' snappy comebacks fer when he meets Joe Keener."

The Bucktails marched until late afternoon and then filed through the Union camp outside Alexandria until they saw their regimental flag flying above Colonel McNeil's headquarters. There Lieutenant Colonel Kane ordered them into parade formation, and the four companies snapped to attention when McNeil appeared from his tent. The sun was knifing through the withdrawing rain clouds, and cheers rose from McNeil's troops when they saw their comrades had returned. After a brief inspection, the colonel dismissed Kane's men by shouting, "Welcome back, Bucktails. Those

Rebs better be wary now that we're together again. Better days are ahead, I can assure you. Fall out now and get reacquainted with your friends."

The next hour was spent shaking hands and swapping pleasantries as the ridge runners from the long separated companies intermingled. When it got to be suppertime, Kane's four companies were ordered to an open field beyond McNeil's portion of camp where they erected their tents. Soon after, two wagon loads of rations were delivered, and Kane's troops feasted in grand style.

"Boy, how long's it been since we had any bacon?" asked Dan, cramming a whole slice into his mouth.

"Too gol-dang long," grunted Sergeant Curtis.

"It's a real blessing to finally have the regiment back together," said Jimmy, gorging on a baked potato.

"I'm jess thankful we'll be gettin' a full night's sleep," yawned Boone. "I can't remember the last time I was this tired."

"I hope you're not comin' down with somethin'," said Bucky.

"There must be somethin' wrong with 'im if he ain't jabberin' like a red squirrel in a tree full o' pine cones," observed Frank.

Reveille wasn't sounded the next morning until the sun was high in the sky. The men woke refreshed from their long sleep, and Lieutenant Colonel Kane led them to a firing range overlooking the Potomac River. There an ordnance wagon was waiting for them, and a squad of United States Sharpshooters collected their muskets in exchange for brand-new Sharps rifles.

"Look at this beauty," said Boone, caressing his new weapon lovingly with his hands. "Why, she's twice as handy as that old Springfield."

"Heck, these Sharps has ta be a whole foot shorter than them muskets, an' breech-loadin' ta boot," enthused Frank.

"This rifle will be lighter to carry, too," added Jimmy. "That's going to make my back real happy."

"I only hope these Sharps is as accurate as my pa's Kentucky rifle," said Bucky. "Then *I'll* be real happy."

After each of Kane's men had visited the ordnance wagon, a lieutenant from the United States Sharpshooters asked for their attention. "Men," he said, holding up one of the new rifles, "you have been issued a Sharps, which many experts believe is the best single-shot breechloader available today. It's safe and reliable and combines accuracy with rapidity. Believe me when I tell you, it's the perfect weapon for skirmishers."

"Excuse me, sir," interrupted Dan Lemon, "but what do we load these here rifles with?"

"What you'll be using, Private, are .52 caliber linen-cased combustible cartridges that are inserted into the chamber. The chamber is opened by pulling down on the trigger guard like so. There'll be no more fiddling with ramrods and Minie balls for you boys. You'll be able to shoot four times faster than with a musket. Just think of the damage you'll do, with the way you Bucktails handle a rifle."

Ten rounds of ammunition were handed out to each Bucktail by members of the lieutenant's squad, who helped Bucky and his friends become familiar with their Sharps. Targets were set up, and each soldier was allowed sight-in time to get a feel for his new weapon.

"Boy, I can't wait ta draw a bead on them Rebs with this!" exclaimed Frank, after firing a few rounds.

"They shoot right where they's aimed, alright," grinned Bucky.

"They also sight in quickly," said Jimmy, "and they're so easy to load. Lying on my belly, I can insert another shell just by moving my hand. I don't have to crawl to my knees or stand up to work the ramrod like I did with the musket. That should cut down on our chances of getting wounded."

"Yep, the lieutenant was right," agreed Curtis. "With these rifles, we's gonna do some serious damage ta the gol-dang Rebs."

Kane's men took turns practicing with their Sharps for the rest of the morning and then returned to camp to find the paymaster waiting with their back-wages. "I think they musta moved up Christmas," chuckled Boone as a clerk counted silver dollars into his waiting hand.

"Yes sir-ee," yelled Frank. "That's what the first farmer I meet's gonna yell when I use this here money ta buy me a big old ham an' some bread that ain't loaded with weevils."

"I'll let the army feed me," grunted Hosea Curtis. "I'm gonna go on over ta McNeil's camp fer an afternoon o' gamblin'. You boys wanna come along?"

"Sure," said Boone. "It'd be a real pleasure ta watch ya lose all yer money. Come on, Bucky. Jimmy. You boys might learn somethin'."

Sergeant Curtis and his squad sauntered across a parade ground and into the clump of tents occupied by McNeil's six companies. It didn't take them long to find a group of soldiers crowded around a rubber blanket laid on the ground. The blanket had different numbers on it. The men placed their money on these numbers while another fellow threw the dice.

"Come join our Chuck-or-Luck band," invited the dice thrower. "Lucky-lookin' fellas like you is bound ta win."

"I'll have a try," said Curtis, laying a pile of coins on the number thirteen. "What about you, Bucky?"

"I'm savin' my money. Sendin' it ta Jimmy's ma."

"Jimmy?"

"Sorry. My religion doesn't permit gambling."

"Frank?"

"I'm buyin' food. Don't ya remember, Sergeant?"

"Boone?"

"Sorry, Hosea, but Chuck-or-Luck's got a bad reputation."

"Why's that?"

"It's known fer keepin' more men on their knees than all the chaplains in this here army."

"The heck with you boys. Roll them dice."

Bucky and his friends watched with a mixture of amusement and dismay as Sergeant Curtis' pile of money grew, then shrank, then grew, then shrank, and disappeared altogether in the course of ten minutes. When Curtis rose cursing from his knees, Frank asked, "Why in blazes did ya bet yer pile on such a number as thirteen? I'd jess as soon break a mirror er deliberately step between a she bear an' her cubs."

"Well, boys, it's like this," groaned the sergeant. "I always pick thirteen 'cause us Bucktails is known as the 1st Rifles er 13th Reserve. With two dice, there was no sense pickin' number *one*."

"Usin' logic like that," laughed Boone, "you'da been better off blowin' yer money on corn liquor."

Curtis' squad had just started back to their own part of camp when a giant man with a shock of unruly, red hair sticking out from beneath his cap came striding up to the sergeant and clamped him roughly in a bear hug that would have broken most men's ribs. "How ya doin' there, Hosea?" bellowed the big ox. "I ain't seen ya in a coon's age."

"Boys," wheezed Curtis when the powerful man released him, "I'd like ya ta meet Joe Keener."

Bucky and Jimmy's eyes got big as cannon balls while Frank backed away from Keener like he was a gorilla that had escaped from a zoo. Only Boone stood his ground and said, "Glad ta finally meet ya, Joe. You're a big un. I didn't think manure could be piled that high."

The huge man's eyes narrowed dangerously, and a growl rumbled in his throat. All at once he gave Boone a playful slap that knocked him halfway across the road. Afterward, the big lumberjack thundered good-naturedly, "You gotta be Boone 'cause Hosea said you was crazy. Ain't no other monkey-faced private in this army—or any other—would dare sass me like that if he wasn't."

"I think when the war ends, I'm gonna get ya real mad at me, Keener," replied Boone as he rose to his feet and dusted himself off.

"Why's that, little man?"

"'Cause you'd knock me all the way back ta McKean County, an' think o' all the shoe leather I'd save."

"Yeah, but you'd land so hard, it'd take ya twice as long ta climb outta the hole ya made as it would ta walk there."

"I jess wonder how a big fella like you hides on a battlefield. You're wider than any oak tree an' too tall ta hunker behind a fence. That must mean you're dang good at dodgin' bullets."

"I don't have ta dodge 'em, Boone. When this here war started, I ate bullets fer breakfast 'til I de-veloped an immunity to 'em. Ya know. Like some fellas do ta rattlesnake poison."

"Well, Joe, ya got me there," laughed Boone. "But that don't mean I'm surrenderin'. We got a long war ahead o' us, an I'm as full o' wisecracks as most generals are o' hot air."

"Yeah, but at least we kin call a truce long enough fer me ta shake yer hand."

"Sorry, Joe, but I'd rather have Hosea slam my hand in a tavern door than risk that grip o' yers. Why don't we jess exchange salutes an' be done with it?"

Boone's suggestion precipitated a series of slapstick salutes that had the rest of the squad doubled over with laughter. First Boone gave a lopsided salute over the bridge of his nose. Joe answered with an off-center salute to the eye. Then Boone saluted from his Adam's apple and pretended to choke, which caused Joe to salute so hard he knocked off his hat, sending his shock of red hair tumbling down over his eyes.

When Boone bent over and saluted from his rear, Sergeant Curtis wheezed, "That's enough, you two. If we don't separate ya soon, we's gonna be too laughed out ta shoot them new Sharps. Come along, Boone. Let's go have us some grub. See ya in the wash, Joe."

"Okay, Hosea. Don't fergit ta bring yer own soap."

After dinner a bugler blew assembly, and the Bucktails filed into formation on the camp parade ground. When the men had come to attention, Colonel McNeil and Lieutenant Colonel Kane rode among the ranks on their horses to inspect the troops. After the inspection was completed, McNeil bellowed to the men, "At ease, Bucktails. It is with great pleasure that I would like to introduce to you Brigadier General Thomas L. Kane. That's right. Our very own lieutenant colonel has been promoted for the bravery he displayed at Catlett's Station and Bull Run. He would now like to say a few parting words before he leaves to take over his new command. General—."

Thomas Kane saluted the men and said in an emotion-charged voice, "I would like to thank the brave members of Companies C, G, H, and I for their loyalty and spirited fighting. We have come a long way together, both as soldiers and men, and now that it's time to part ways, I want to wish you the best. I know I leave you in the very capable hands of Colonel Hugh McNeil. My promotion is, above all, a testament to the bravery and hard-earned reputation of the entire Bucktail Regiment."

When General Kane finished speaking, the ranks erupted with a chorus of cheers, and many men chanted his name until Kane again saluted the regiment. Then the general reined his horse around and galloped off down the road to Alexandria with his two orderlies, who were hard-pressed to keep up.

As Kane disappeared from sight, Jimmy said to Bucky, "There goes a fine man and an inspirational leader. Without him, the Bucktails will not be the same."

"Maybe not," replied Bucky, "but the fightin' ain't never gonna change. An' us wildcats'll keep clawin' at them Rebs 'til the end."

"But who knows when the gol-dang end will come?" grunted Hosea Curtis. "This here war could keep goin' long enough fer our sons ta be Bucktails. All we kin do is follow orders an' keep fightin' fer whoever's in charge. I heared that Edward Irvin o' Company K is gonna take Kane's place. He's a good man, too."

"I also heared from Captain McDonald's boys that the Rebs is plannin' an in-vasion o' the North," added Boone smugly.

"Oh, Boone," groaned Frank. "Not more rumors from them fellas."

"Yeah, it seems that Lee's victory at Bull Run's got him all charged up, an' he's headin' inta Maryland at this here very minute."

"If that's true," said Jimmy, "we'd better head back to camp and get packing."

"You're right," agreed Bucky. "An' like Colonel McNeil said, them Rebs had better watch out now that us Bucktails is up ta full strength."

"Hey, Bucky, did ya ever get a chance ta give General Kane back his pipe?" asked Boone.

"No, there jess wasn't time."

"Well, Bucky, I wouldn't worry about it too much," assured Jimmy. "Your paths are bound to cross again when we return to Pennsylvania."

The Bucktails march off to Antietam and the bloodiest day of fighting in the Civil War.

Bibliography

Angle, Paul M. *A Pictorial History of the Civil War Years.* Garden City, N.Y.: Doubleday & Company, Inc., 1967.

Arnett, Hazel. *I Hear America Singing.* New York: Praeger Publishers, 1975.

Athearn, Robert G. *The Civil War.* New York: Choice Publishing, Inc., 1988.

Bates, Samuel P. *History of Pennsylvania Volunteers 1861– 1865.* 5 vols. Harrisburg, Pa.: B. Singerly, State Printer, 1869.

———. *Martial Deeds of Pennsylvania.* Philadelphia: T. H. Davis Company, 1876.

Billings, John D. *Hard Tack and Coffee.* Boston: George M. Smith & Co., 1887.

Botkin, B. A., ed. *A Civil War Treasury of Tales, Legends and Folklore.* New York: Random House, 1960.

Bowman, John S., ed. *The Civil War Day by Day.* Greenwich, Conn.: Dorset Press, 1989.

Brandt, Dennis W. "The Bucktail Regiment." *Potter County Historical Society Quarterly Bulletin*, January 1998, pp. 2–3.

Catton, Bruce. *The Army of the Potomac: Mr. Lincoln's Army.* Garden City, N.Y.: Doubleday & Company, Inc., 1962.

Chamberlin, Lieutenant Colonel Thomas. *History of the One Hundred and Fiftieth Regiment Pennsylvania Volunteers, Second Regiment, Bucktail Brigade.* Philadelphia: F. McManus, Jr. & Company, 1905.

Commager, Henry Steele. *The Blue and the Gray.* 2 vols. New York: The Fairfax Press, 1982.

*Glover, Edwin A. *Bucktailed Wildcats: A Regiment of Civil War Volunteers.* New York: Thomas Yoseloff, 1960.

History of the Counties of McKean, Elk, Cameron and Potter, Pennsylvania. 2 vols. Chicago: J. H. Beers & Co. Publishers, 1890.

Leish, Kenneth W., ed. *The American Heritage Songbook.* New York: American Heritage Publishing Company, Inc., 1969.

Lord, Francis A. *Civil War Collector's Encyclopedia.* New York: Castle Books, 1965.

McClellan, Elizabeth. *History of American Costume 1607–1870.* New York: Tudor Publishing Company, 1937.

Nofi, Albert A. *The Civil War Treasury.* New York: Mallard Press, 1990.

O'Shea, Richard. *Battle Maps of the Civil War.* Tulsa: Council Oak Books, 1992.

Stern, Phillip Van Doren, ed. *Soldier Life in the Union and Confederate Armies.* Bloomington: Indiana University Press, 1961.

Stone, Rufus Barrett. *McKean: The Governor's County.* New York: Lewis Historical Publishing Company, Inc., 1926.

Sutherland, Daniel E. *The Expansion of Everyday Life 1860–1876.* New York: Harper & Row Publishers, 1989.

Tanner, Robert G. *Stonewall in the Valley.* Garden City, N.Y.: Doubleday & Company, Inc., 1976.

*Thomson, O. R. Howard, and William H. Rauch. *History of the Bucktails.* Philadelphia: Electric Printing Company, 1906.

The Union Army. 8 vols. Madison, Wisc.: Federal Publishing Company, 1908.

Ward, Geoffrey C. *The Civil War: An Illustrated History.* New York: Alfred A. Knopf, Inc., 1990.

Warner, Ezra J. *Generals in Blue.* Baton Rouge: Louisiana State University Press, 1964.

Wilcox, R. Turner. *Five Centuries of American Costume.* New York: Charles Scribner's Sons, 1963.

* These sources provided the portions of dialogue attributed to real-life officers that appear in *The Bucktails' Shenandoah March.*

Also by
the Authors

The story of Bucky's and Jimmy's lives prior to their enlistment in the Bucktail Regiment and their adventures as recruits.

Hayfoot, Strawfoot: The Bucktail Recruits

When Bucky and Jimmy enlisted in Colonel Thomas Kane's Bucktail Regiment at Smethport, Pennsylvania, in April of 1861, they had no idea of the dangers they would endure before they ever plunged into battle. An encounter with a den of timber rattlers, a wild raft ride down a whitewater river, and a fight-to-the-death with a murderous lumberjack recruit were just a few of the pitfalls dotting their path to war. Hardened by these adversities, the boys go on to prove their mettle at the Battle of Dranesville.

Hayfoot, Strawfoot: The Bucktail Recruits is a must read for anyone who enjoys historical fiction, the Civil War, and action-packed adventure. Researched from the double perspectives of history and folklore, this book gives a vivid account of the birth of a famous Union rifle regiment and the coming of age of two young frontier recruits.

Robertson and Rimer enlist the reader to join two innocent boys from a backwater hamlet marching off to the turmoil of the American Civil War. One is a rough-hewn child of the outdoors, and the other a pampered preacher's son. They quickly bond to face the pain of adolescence, the rigors of army life, the sting of prejudice, and the hope for glory.

ISBN 1-57249-250-3
$7.95